# Love, Planes, & Heartache

A gay love story

## Lee Quail

# Table of Contents


Six Years Later .................................................................. 1

Chapter 1 .......................................................................... 3

Chapter 2 ......................................................................... 13

Chapter 3 ......................................................................... 19

Chapter 4 ......................................................................... 23

Chapter 5 ......................................................................... 31

Chapter 6 ......................................................................... 33

Chapter 7 ......................................................................... 37

Chapter 8 ......................................................................... 41

Chapter 9 ......................................................................... 51

Chapter 10 ........................................................................ 55

Chapter 11 ........................................................................ 61

Chapter 12 ........................................................................ 65

Chapter 13 ........................................................................ 69

Chapter 14 ........................................................................ 71

Chapter 15 ........................................................................ 75

Chapter 16 ........................................................................ 79

Chapter 17 ........................................................................ 83

Chapter 18 ........................................................................ 91

Chapter 19 ........................................................................ 93

Chapter 20 ........................................................................ 99

Chapter 21 ....................................................................... 109

Chapter 22 ....................................................................... 115

Chapter 23 ....................................................................... 117

Chapter 24 ....................................................................... 127

Chapter 25 ....................................................................... 133

Chapter 26 ....................................................................... 135

Chapter 27 ....................................................................... 139

3 Months Later .................................................................. 141

Epilogue ......................................................................... 151

Find me online: ................................................................. 155

Dedication ....................................................................... 157

Healing means finding the courage to create new moments of joy

# Prologue

## 6 Years Earlier

Mike tentatively extended a hand toward the sleeping figure beside him. He hesitated for a moment, then gently shook the man's shoulder. He swatted Mike's hand away with a faint, irritated murmur.

Undeterred, Mike leaned closer, his voice urgent. "Philip, wake up," he urged, his words a soft but insistent plea. His fingers brushed against Philip's arm. "I think we have a problem."

"What's going on?" Philip said, concerned.

"I had a dream. I was in your mom's house talking to her, and then suddenly there was this sudden flash of light and she disappeared. I think you should call her and make sure she's okay."

"It's two-thirty in the morning, babe," Philip replied, still groggy.

"Please, just call her," Mike insisted. The vividness of his dream, coupled with the urgency he felt upon waking, had left him unsettled. Despite the late hour and Philip's grogginess, Mike's concern for June's well-being was paramount, even more so than his own tiredness.

Philip hesitated, looking sceptical. "Do you really believe in that stuff?"

Mike's expression was serious. "I don't know, When I woke up I had this sense of loss. It felt so real. Just for my peace of mind, will you please call her?"

Philip sighed, "I'll give her a quick call."

Philip pressed his mother's number into his mobile phone and waited for an answer.

"Philip. This is an odd time to call," June, his mother answered.

Relieved, Philip responded, "Hey, Mom. Sorry for waking you. Mike just had a strange dream, and is worried. Are you okay?"

She chuckled, "Oh, sweetie. I'm perfectly fine, don't you worry. Just a bit groggy from being woken up. Tell Mike not to stress."

Philip's tension eased as he heard his mother's reassuring words. "Thanks. I'll let him know. Sorry again for waking you."

"No problem, dear," she replied warmly.

Turning to Mike, seated with his knees pressed up against his chin, Philip said, "She's alright. Just a little sleepy."

Mike's relief was palpable as he nodded, "That's good to know." A small smile tugged at the corners of his lips. "I was worried something might have happened to her."

Philip's voice held a touch of affection as he suggested, "Now, let's get some sleep. Tomorrow's a long day."

As they settled in, ready to drift off, Mike offered a light-hearted explanation for his earlier distress. "Maybe it's those muscle relaxant tabs," he mused.

"How many did you take?" Philip said.

"Three."

"Three? Your dosage is one every night."

"One doesn't help. Two is mild. Three puts me to sleep."

"You're flying out in a few hours to meet with Lauren, will you be okay?"

Mike sighed and closed his eyes, hoping the drowsiness would overcome him despite the unsettling thoughts that circled his mind. "I'll be okay."

Philip turned onto his side, eyeing Mike with concern. "You know, it's not healthy to rely on those tabs so heavily. You've been taking them since we moved here."

"Everything here in Cape Town is so rushed. It's like life is stuck in a speed frame of a movie."

Philip nodded, understanding the pressures they both faced in their demanding jobs. Philip planned weddings and Mike flew a light plane. "Well, maybe after this meeting with Lauren, you can take some time to focus on your well-being. She's a valuable client, but your health should come first."

"You're right," Mike conceded. "I'll talk to her about possibly rescheduling some upcoming projects. I need to get this sleep thing under control."

"I would have gone with you if it weren't for the UNESCO celebration starting tomorrow."

"Someone has to be there running the show," Mike said. "You don't have to shoulder everything yourself. We're a team, and we should be able to rely on each other."

Philip nodded, "I appreciate that. It's just... I've always been the one to handle these things."

"You said you wanted to bring Emma on board. Any progress there?"

Philip shifted slightly. "I've been in touch with her, and she seems interested."

Mike's tired eyes brightened. "That's good to hear. Emma is sharp, and her organizational skills are top-notch. Having her share the load might just be what we need."

"I think so too," Mike agreed. "Her perspective is fresh, and she's not afraid to challenge the status quo. Plus, she's familiar with the kind of work we do. Now, let's both try to get some rest."

As they settled in for the night, the weight of their responsibilities still hung in the air, but it felt somehow more manageable with the prospect of Emma's potential involvement. They settled into a comfortable silence, the room lit only by the soft glow of the white moon and the sound of waves lapping the shore, and soon both men fell asleep in each other's arms.

****

The small airport buzzed with activity beneath the bright morning sun. Mike stood proudly beside his beloved Cessna 172. It was a crisp, perfect day for flying, and he felt the thrill of the open skies calling.

As the Cessna rolled onto the runway, Mike's confidence shone through. He was an experienced pilot who felt at home in the sky. He held the control yoke firmly with gloved hands, feeling every little movement. He double-checked everything, listening to the engine's RPMs, smelling the familiar aviation fuel. He made sure the fuel selector was in the right position just by touch. He looked at the electrical meter to ensure everything worked fine, and he adjusted the radios and controls with his fingertips. His eyes scanned the warning lights to catch any issues. He paid close attention to the flight instruments, feeling the yoke's movements as he checked the airspeed, altitude, and other important details. He even closed his eyes briefly to mentally prepare for take-off, picturing the whole process in his mind. Eventually, he tapped the radio button and announced: "Tower, this is Mike Bravo Charlie Alpha 172, ready for take-off on Runway Four. Requesting clearance for departure."

The tower responded briskly, crackling over the radio: "Mike Bravo Charlie Alpha 172, Tower here. You are cleared for take-off on Runway Four. Wind is north-easterly and calm. Maintain runway heading and altitude until further advised."

Mike acknowledged: "Roger, Tower. Cleared for take-off on Runway Four. Will maintain runway heading and altitude. Mike Bravo Charlie Alpha 172, out."

As Mike taxied the Cessna onto the runway, adrenaline coursing through him. The engines roared with anticipation as he advanced the throttle. The Cessna surged forward, accelerating down the runway. The sensation of speed built with every passing second.

He kept a steady hand on the control yoke, feeling the power of the plane beneath him. The world outside became a blur, and the runway stretched out before him. With a final check of his instruments, Mike eased the control yoke back, and the Cessna responded, gracefully leaving the ground. The runway fell away below him, and he was no longer bound to the earth.

Stealing a glance to his right, the tower stood as a distant sentinel. He was airborne. With every passing moment, the worries of the ground melted away, and he was one with the sky, climbing over Devil's Peak.

The Cessna sliced through the sky, but then, like a bolt from the blue, chaos erupted. Warning lights blared crimson, and shrill alarms pierced the air as the horizontal stabiliser control malfunctioned, shattering the peace.

Mike's brow furrowed in disbelief. "What the fuck!"

His heart raced, but he couldn't panic. With a surge of adrenaline he wrestled the control yoke, fighting to regain control. The aircraft wobbled and threatened to tilt dangerously.

Desperately, Mike throttled back, slowing the aircraft's furious ascent. His gloved hands trembled as he scrutinized the trim settings, praying for divine intervention.

Amid the frantic alarms, he locked eyes on the flight instruments, the altitude indicator guiding his every move. "Mayday! Mayday!" he called desperately into the radio. "Stabilizer's shot. I'm losing control!"

Above the tumultuous symphony of alarms and rattling controls, Mike lost his steely resolve. "This can't be happening!" Sweat trickled down his temple as he wrestled with the control yoke, his muscles straining against the defiant machine. The Cessna wobbled and tilted dangerously. Mike's hands quivered as he fought to level the aircraft. "You can do this," he whispered, gritting his teeth. "You've got this!"

In the face of Mike's distress call and the unfolding emergency, ground control leaped into action. "172, this is Ground Control. We hear your distress call. Stay calm. Please confirm your current altitude and position?"

"Ground Control, this is 172. I'm at 3,000 feet, approximately 10 km's northwest of the airport."

"Copy, 172. We're tracking your position. We're here to assist. First, can you attempt to reset the stabilizer control as per your aircraft's emergency procedures?"

"Roger that, Ground Control. Initiating reset now... No response, the stabilizer is still malfunctioning!"

"Understood, 172. We're declaring an emergency. You are cleared for an immediate return to the airport. Fly heading 180 to initiate your turn back to the runway."

Determined, Mike responded with; "Heading 180...Oh my God..."

"Mike Bravo Charlie Alpha 172, this is Ground Control. We've lost contact with you. Please respond. Over."

No response. Just static.

"All units, we have a potential emergency. Mike Bravo Charlie Alpha 172 has lost contact. Initiating emergency response protocol. Notify emergency services and dispatch search and rescue teams immediately. Get eyes on the last known position. Mike Bravo Charlie Alpha 172, if you can hear this message, transmit your location. Over..."

Silence.

# Six Years Later

1

# Chapter 1

Dressed to the nines in a three-piece black suit, Philip Mitchell resembled a wedding-planning ninja on a mission. With his trusty clipboard as the weapon of choice, he prowled through the venue like a graceful gazelle, making sure every detail was absolutely perfect. His obsession with precision was on a whole new level. He'd fuss over chairs and benches like a hyperactive interior decorator, making tiny adjustments to ensure the seating arrangements were as straight as a ruler. If he had a measuring tape for every blade of grass, he'd probably be on his knees in the sprawling garden.

As the guests started trickling in, Philip's ordinary demeanour melted away, replaced by an aura of warmth and charisma. He embraced each person as if they were cherished companions he hadn't seen in ages. He seamlessly guided each individual to their designated seat. His movements were graceful, with a gentle touch and a friendly word, he made everyone feel not just welcomed, but truly cherished.

He had created an environment where strangers became friends, and he hoped that one day his own life could match the perfectly orchestrated event of his cousin's wedding.

He possessed a peculiar love-hate relationship with weddings. He had to put on a big smile and pretend to love all the frilly dresses and over-the-top decorations, and today was no different.

But, deep down, he had a secret dream — to become a published writer. He yearned to see his name in print and have his words touch the hearts of readers everywhere. Unfortunately, his writing career was about as non-existent as the Loch Ness monster. He fantasised about book signings and movie deals while helping couples choose between white or ivory tablecloths. It was a comedy of contradictions, like trying to decide between chocolate cake and an alpha-male's six-pack. He had to pay the bills somehow, and those extravagant weddings weren't going to plan themselves. Until his writing breakthrough finally arrived, he would keep pinning corsages and penning love stories in his mind. After all, every great writer had to start somewhere, even if it was in the world of satin bows and flower arrangements.

Little did he know that fate had something extraordinary in store for him in the sea of bouquets and satin ribbons. But for now, he was on a mission to make Barbara's big day unforgettable, even if it meant risking a few wrinkles from all the chair-adjusting acrobatics. And, just as he was about to congratulate himself on a job well done, a familiar voice issued from behind him.

His mother.

June wrapped him in a proud mama bear hug. "Oh, Philip, everything is perfectly perfect," she exclaimed, her brown eyes sparkling with joy.

Grinning from ear to ear, Philip whispered, "Mom, you look more stunning than the bride."

June playfully waved off his praise. "Charmer! You always say the nicest things," she chuckled.

Her warm presence radiated love and her soft, compassionate eyes held the wisdom of a thousand lifetimes.

Philip's fingers danced along the strands of her hair. "And your hair looks amazing."

But it was the necklace that caught Philip's attention — an exquisite piece with a dazzling, crimson ruby. He couldn't tear his eyes away from its vibrant allure. "Grandma's ruby necklace, it's absolutely stunning."

Blushing, June said, "Thank you, my dear boy. I haven't worn it since my own wedding last century sometime."

Concerned, Philip asked, "Where's Dad?"

"You know your father. Weddings and funerals aren't his cup of tea. Gone fishing with that man from Spain."

"Wait, you travelled all the way from Cape Point by yourself?"

A mischievous smile appeared on June's lightly coloured red lips as she extended her hand towards the man standing behind her. "No, not alone. I want you to meet Richard Moore, a dear friend. He's my handsome chaperone for the day."

Richard stepped forward with a self-assured smile and Philip's heart did a happy dance. The way the man carried himself exuded confidence, from his perfectly styled fair hair and golden moustache that merged perfectly with a trimmed, designed beard, to the diamond translucence in his eyes.

June interjected with a laugh. "Richard wears cotton trousers and a tie to work, but when it comes to weddings, he's all about jeans, no socks, a cotton jacket, and a t-shirt. I'll never understand you youngsters no matter how I try."

Richard chimed in; his voice filled with bubbly enthusiasm. "Funerals too, don't forget! I don't wear socks to funerals." His voice flowed like a gentle stream, its clarity shimmered through the air like sunlight dancing on water.

Their hands met in a firm handshake, sending an electric current racing through Philip's veins. "Thanks for accompanying my mom. I hope you enjoy the wedding."

Richard chuckled, his silver eyes twinkling mischievously. "Honestly, I'm not the biggest fan of weddings."

Philip nodded, "Well, I appreciate you being here for my mom. Maybe you'll at least enjoy the food!"

Richard grinned, "I'll make the most of it."

Standing in the presence of such a man felt like a symphony of butterflies tangled in the garden of Philip's thoughts. He had to make a quick getaway or he'd end up embarrassing himself completely. "I had better get back to work. Looks like Barbara has arrived," he said, ready to dive into his duties.

"Go, do your thing, dear!" June exclaimed, waving him off with a flurry of her hand.

Philip turned stiffly. What the hell is going on with you, Philip Mitchell? You're shaking! he thought, rushing towards the bride. Just take it easy. Signals can be misleading. On his way he turned to take one more peek at the man he had just met. Richard had taken June's elbow, guiding her towards the table reserved for them, and to Philip's surprise, Richard glanced back, just for a moment.

Philip looked away immediately. Too late! Before he could regain his composure, he unexpectedly bumped into a table, prompting a glass to teeter and tumble. It clinked softly before making a swift descent to the floor, where it shattered into tiny fragments. Philip's fingers fumbled as he hastened to retrieve the shattered glass. When he looked up, Richard was there with him, on his haunches, collecting the shards of glass too. His kind eyes twinkled with empathy, and a genuine smile graced his lips. "My fault," Richard said, his voice carrying a hint of amusement.

Philip looked somewhat embarrassed but managed to force a smile. "It's okay, really. I wasn't thinking clearly," he admitted. His heart raced, threatening to burst from his chest as he locked eyes with Richard. With gentle care, Richard took the remaining glass from Philip's hand. "Thanks," Philip murmured. "I'll have someone clean up the rest of this mess."

Richard said, "Accidents happen, and it's all under control now."

Philip nodded appreciatively, feeling a sense of relief from Richard's calm demeanour. "I'd best get to the bride. She looks nervous."

Barbara, at the entrance, wearing a flowing white gown, stood beside her bridesmaids, all dressed in cheerful yellow. She tightly held onto a deep red rose, a vibrant contrast to the elegance of her filigree wedding dress.

Philip made his way toward Barbara, weaving his way between tables and chairs, careful not to bump another glass off a table.

Barbara's eyes brightened as Philip approached, and her nervousness seemed to dissipate momentarily. "Philip, I'm so nervous," she said. "Everything's been a whirlwind, and I can't believe the time has finally come."

Philip returned her smile, his own unease momentarily forgotten. "You look absolutely stunning, Barbara. This is your day, and it's going to be perfect."

Her grip on the red rose relaxed. "I hope so. But I must admit, the jitters are getting the best of me."

Philip chuckled warmly. "It's only natural. Remember, this is a celebration of your love and happiness. Just take a deep breath, watch out for the thorns on that stem, and everything will fall into place. James is ready and waiting, and nervous," he chuckled, straightening out her short veil. Her fiancé waited at the end of the aisle and ran a hand through his hair, straightened his black bowtie, and took a deep breath.

"I'm just waiting for Daddy. Thank you for all this, Philip," Barbara said.

"It's my pleasure," Philip said, gently pressing his lips to her hand. "And look, here comes your dad." He turned, gracefully navigating his way toward the band stationed beside the podium. As he passed by Richard's table, a warmth spread across his face as he caught sight of Richard's approving smile and a subtle nod of encouragement. Philip's heart swelled with a renewed sense of confidence as he took his place beside the musicians, ready to accompany Barbara on her journey down the aisle.

Philip exchanged a final reassuring glance with Richard before his fingers graced the keys of the piano, sending forth a melodic prelude that set the tone for Barbara's grand entrance.

Everyone turned their attention to the entrance as Barbara's father walked her down the aisle and the guests fell silent as they reached the podium and her father handed her over to James.

While the ceremony continued in the background, Philip visited the kitchen, nervously tasting all the food on the menu. Everything was going according to plan. It was the unplanned moment of meeting Richard that made him nervous. He just made it back to the ceremony in time to see the happy couple exchange vows. Their promises resonated through the gathering, solidifying their commitment for all eternity. They exchanged rings and finally the pastor announced, "Ladies and gentlemen, I present to you, Mr. and Mrs. James McMurdo!"

The celebration moved to a nearby reception area, and the newlyweds took to the dance floor. They moved gracefully together as the band played a waltz, each step exuded tenderness — and practised perfection.

Throughout the evening, Philip stole glances at Richard's table, yearning for another smile, but Richard seemed oblivious, not even batting an eyelid in Philip's direction. Had Philip misread the signs? Had his gaydar malfunctioned? The realisation hit him like a runaway freight train that Richard could be straight! All those electric sparks were nothing more than a figment of Philip's overactive imagination.

He resigned himself to the possibility that Richard had no interest in him and drowned his sorrows at the open bar, hoping that the bottom of his glass would hold the answers to his non-existent love life. Despite the vibrant atmosphere and the festivities that surrounded him, he couldn't shake off the melancholy that settled in his chest and alcohol didn't help at all.

He craved a moment away from the crowd and stepped out onto the balcony, the warm night air caressing his skin. His eyes fixated on the fountain in the garden below. As he stood there, lost in his one-sided contemplation of Richard, a voice crackled behind him, breaking the rushing sound of water.

He turned around. It was Emma with a mischievous grin on her face. "When are you going to find someone to settle down with?" she asked, raising an eyebrow.

Philip's shoulders slumped. "Maybe I should start a support group for unwanted men or something."

Emma chuckled and patted Philip on the back. "Not just men. Count me in too. I've had my fair share of crushes on men who couldn't even remember my name. We'll call it, the 'Perpetually Single' club."

Philip laughed, the heaviness in his heart momentarily lifted. "That's actually not a bad idea. We'll have membership cards, matching t-shirts, and a secret handshake. We'll make being perpetually single a fashion statement."

Emma's friendship and the ability to find humour in their romantic misadventures were the true treasures in his life. As they continued to joke, Philip knew that even if Richard never saw him again, he had a friend in Emma who cherished him. And maybe, just maybe, the right person would come along one day when he least expected it, ready to appreciate his charm and magnetism — gaydar malfunction or not.

"I best go back to my table," Emma said. "Maybe a lost bachelor will ask me for a dance or offer me a couple of gins. Like I'm so available and no one even knows it. Who is that man with your mother? He's absolutely gorgeous. He's been watching you."

"Richard? Watching me? I've been trying to catch his attention the whole night!"

"The moment you turn your back he watches you. He's been watching your every move."

"Really? Probably a heartbreaker."

"You won't know if you don't do something, Philip. Go talk to him."

"Maybe later."

"You always say that but later comes and goes. It's not like you've got men lining up to date you."

"I don't want men lining up anyway. I'm quite happy the way I am."

Emma lightly touched his chin. "Are you really happy?"

He didn't answer, instead he looked away from her at a couple kissing in the garden below.

"Oh, and by the way, well done," she said, giving him a nod of approval. "You really outdid yourself with this event. Everyone's buzzing about it."

Philip smiled, appreciating the recognition. "I couldn't have done it without your help. You're a superstar."

As Emma made her way towards the door, she paused and turned. "I think I found a publisher for your work. We'll discuss it tomorrow."

Philip's face lit up. "You're the best." He waved goodbye as she disappeared into the bustling crowd.

He leaned against the balustrade. The vibrant sounds of the party faded into the background as he closed his eyes and whispered, "Richard's watching you? How could you have missed it? You're such a klutz, Philip Mitchell. The man of your dreams is right here and you're scared as usual. If you don't get it together, you'll turn into a grumpy old man and regret this day...."

"And he plays the piano...."

Taking a deep breath, Philip opened his eyes and spun around.

"Richard!"

"I need some fresh air and it's too noisy in there," Richard said, walking towards him.

"It's hot in there, I also needed some fresh air." Philip replied.

"Your mom tells me you planned this whole wedding from start to finish. Well done, it's awesome."

"That's not entirely true. I have a partner, Emma. She also had a hand in it."

A momentary silence followed. "Your mom told me you're writing a book."

"It's nearly finished."

"I'd love to read it sometime."

Philip hesitated, contemplating the offer. "It's semi-autobiographical, and a lot of it is boring."

"Well, if you ever need a beta reader, let me know. I'll gladly help out."

"Thank you. Are you enjoying yourself?" Philip asked.

A faint smile appeared on Richard's lips, the same smile he had displayed earlier. "Now I am, yes."

"Only now?"

"I'm not a great socializer. I teach twelfth grade English, so I get my fair share of crowds and cheeky students."

"I see now why you offered to read my work."

"Richard! There you are!" June stepped out onto the balcony, interrupting them. "I've been looking all over for you." She took both men by the elbow and escorted them inside. "It's almost midnight and the happy couple are about to say goodbye. We're supposed to form an arch to cheer them on their way."

All the guests lined up opposite their partners, forming a human tunnel with their hands raised high above their shoulders. June, ever mischievous, seized the opportunity to play matchmaker and pushed Richard towards the line, conveniently placing him opposite Philip.

As Philip's hands touched Richard's, his heart performed a wild percussion solo, thumping against his ribcage like an over-enthusiastic drummer, and when their gaze met, Philip was captivated. Time slowed, and all he could focus on were Richard's silver eyes. It was as if a gravitational force had pulled him closer.

At last, the clock struck midnight and the married couple negotiated the tunnel while everyone sang, 'A Thousand Miles', except for Philip and Richard who were too busy staring at each other.

Philip revelled in the warmth of Richard's gaze spreading through his entire body and he wondered if Richard was experiencing the same sensation, or thinking of going home. Cheers and wolf whistles went up from the rowdy guests as the newly married couple passed under their hands. Philip snapped back to reality, blushing furiously as he quickly withdrew his hand from Richard's.

It was close to one in the morning, and exhaustion clung to Philip like a relentless partygoer who just wouldn't take the hint to leave. His head throbbed with pain, and his legs felt like they had run a marathon. The late hour seemed to stretch on endlessly, and he yearned for the comfort of his bed, but sleep felt like a distant luxury, teasingly out of reach. He couldn't shake off the fatigue that weighed him down with every step, turning his usual light stride into a sluggish shuffle. All he wanted was to sleep. As he stood in the kitchen, supervising the equally tired but determined washing staff, June found him, wearing the exhaustion on his face like a badge of honour.

"It was a lovely wedding," June said, planting a kiss on his cheek. "I'm leaving for Cape Point quite early. See you Tuesday?"

Philip mustered a weary smile. "As usual I'll be there. Where's Richard?" he said, looking around as if expecting Richard to magically materialise out of thin air.

"Off getting the car," June said. "Any message for him?"

Philip pondered for a moment, "No message. Take care, Mom. Have a safe trip." He watched June leave the kitchen, and regretted not saying goodbye to Richard. It felt like an opportunity had slipped away, a chance to express his gratitude for escorting his mother, and perhaps even hint at a desire for something more than fleeting glances across a crowded room and an unfinished conversation on a balcony.

He locked the kitchen, ready to finally call it a night, reminding himself that life was unpredictable, and perhaps one day, when he least expected it, the universe would sprinkle a little magic into his own love story.

# Chapter 2

The following morning, just before eight, Philip slumped his way to his front door where Emma waited, looking as if she had slept for a week. Philip didn't feel the same and she understood the toll weddings took on his spirit.

"Hey, Emma," he greeted, his words accompanied by a slight yawn. Her vibrant personality lit up the room. Long, chestnut hair cascaded in loose waves around her shoulders, framing a face with sparkling hazel eyes that danced with mischief. She had been a pillar of support in Philip's life, always there to lend an empathetic ear and offer guidance. With a gentle touch and compassionate heart, she understood him on a level few others could.

"Congratulations on another perfect event for Barbara and James," she said, heading straight for the patio facing the beach. The waves broke gently along the wide and sandy beach. The water sparkled under the sun while seagulls flew low in search of small fish or shiny shells. "They couldn't get hold of you, so they reached out to me. They were absolutely thrilled with everything."

He smiled, "I just wish I had a "wedding recovery" button to press, you know, like the ones they have on microwaves."

Emma burst into laughter. "A wedding recovery button? Imagine just pressing it and instantly feeling refreshed and ready for the next event."

"It would be the new must-have gadget for wedding planners worldwide!"

Emma, perceptive as ever, noticed the fatigue and unspoken sadness in his voice. She swiftly diverted the conversation. "You seem sad. Have you been thinking about Mike again?"

"Mike? No. I'm just tired. If only yawning burned calories, I'd be a fitness model by now."

"And Richard?"

"What about him?"

"Did you guys connect?"

Philip poured water into a glass kettle for coffee and placed it on the gas stove. "If you can call a broken glass and a one-minute conversation on the balcony, a connection, yes. Otherwise, no. He didn't even say goodbye. Maybe I need a "how to make lasting connections" handbook."

Emma giggled. "That's a bummer," she said. "And I guess you didn't give him your number?"

"I've been out of circulation for six years, Em. Phone numbers, addresses, dates. They're all foreign to me. I don't even know what it's like to kiss a guy anymore. I'm practically an ancient relic in the dating world."

"Oh, come on now! You're not that old. You just need some romantic rejuvenation!"

"Is that like a fountain of youth for love?"

"You bet! You take a dip in it, and suddenly, you're bursting with charm and confidence! I'm telling you, it's the next big anti-aging trend! If I had met him, and if he was straight, he'd be in my bed right now, but you know that I don't waste time."

"Don't remind me. I know how you move." Suddenly, Philip's eyes clouded over with sadness. "I didn't get to the cemetery this last week."

"You must feel terrible. I don't know what it's like to lose true love like that, but I imagine I would also keep the memory alive."

"I try."

"I'm sorry, babe. Back to what I wanted to say. I'm glad you finally noticed a man."

"Still doesn't make it right."

"It's a step in the right direction."

"I promised Mike to never fall in love again."

"I know. And I think that was foolish of you. You can't stop love. It's like water, it always finds a way."

Philip's gaze dropped to the ground as he pondered her words, his heart heavy with the weight of his past and the uncertain future ahead. The waves crashing nearby seemed to echo the ebb and flow of his emotions, a constant reminder of the unpredictable journey of love and healing.

"Change of subject. There's a new book out by Grey Mattison, and it's making waves. The critics are raving about it."

Philip's interest piqued. "Really? What's it called?"

"The Invincible Charm of a Romantic Magician."

"That's some title," he laughed. "Who's the publisher?"

"Bolt Publishing. Apparently, they have a knack for discovering talented authors. I researched them online and guess what? They are looking for unsolicited romantic material, fiction and non-fiction between forty and fifty-thousand words. They're looking for an uber-romantic gay love story because, apparently, South Africa doesn't have a mainstream writer who writes gay romances. Have you finished it?"

Philip had heard of Bolt Publishing. A reputable publisher known for exceptional romance novels. His face lit up with a rough replica of the Giaconda smile "It's finished."

"Time to send out that query letter," Emma said.

"We?"

"Us. You and me. Today. Now."

"I haven't even thought about the query letter, or the synopsis. Putting a manuscript of 80,000 words into 500 words or less isn't easy. Some publishers want taglines – others want each chapter outlined, and some want three chapters or one chapter or the whole book. It's so confusing."

Emma booted up her laptop and Philip settled down beside her.

"I've got Bolt's website on screen now. All they want is a cover letter with a one-page synopsis, your bio, and the first three chapters. Seems easy enough."

"When I stumbled upon Bolt Publishing, I knew it was the perfect opportunity for you."

"What can I say? I didn't think anyone would be interested in my boring story."

"It's actually quite beautiful. How do you want readers to feel about your novel?"

"I want them to feel the magnetic pull between Mike and Philip."

"What about emphasizing the contrasting worlds they come from. This is a story of an events planner and a divorced grocery store owner challenging themselves and finding a connection with each other."

They spent the next hour refining the cover letter, carefully selecting words that would captivate the publisher's attention and Philip's distinctive storytelling style. In the final version of the cover letter, Philip's vision for "Final Flight" had finally found its voice.

"Happy?" Emma asked.

"Blown away. Now for the synopsis."

She presented him with a small file she had brought with her.

"What's this?" he asked, taking it from her.

"I read every word of your novel, and I made notes on each chapter," she said, pointing to the file. "I think we should use those notes to shape the synopsis. We can write several synopses: a long one, detailing every chapter, or a short one and a blurb. What do you think?"

Philip nodded, appreciating Emma's thoroughness and dedication. "Sounds great. You seem to know more about the business of writing than me."

After careful consideration, they introduced the main characters, outlined the central conflict, and highlighted the key turning points and emotional arcs in the novel. By the time they completed the task, they had a meticulously polished one-page synopsis that painted a vivid picture of Mike and Philip's journey and their challenges.

"That leaves us with your bio," Emma said. "Now, please don't be angry with me, but I took the liberty to draft a three-hundred-word bio for you. Take a look."

"I mean a bio is kind of personal," Philip reminded her.

"I know. But you are lazy so I did it for you."

*Philip Mitchell lives in a small suburb of Cape Town called Llandudno and writes every day, even if it is just half a page. He specializes in feel-good romances that immerse the reader in situations that are compelling and heartfelt from the very first word. He is also a Wedding Planner and has written extensively on how to create the perfect wedding event - all self-published. When he's not writing or being a true romantic, he spends time with his loyal best friend, and business partner, Emma. "Final Flight" is his debut novel.*

"Looks good to me," Philip said.

"You're not angry?"

"Why, should I be?"

"I thought there might be an inaccuracy, especially the part about me being your loyal, best friend. People will think I'm a dog."

"Well, you can be at times," Philip laughed.

Emma smacked him on his head. "Bitch! How can you say that?"

"It's the truth."

"My bark is worse than my bite," she said, smiling.

"Where are they situated? The publishers," he inquired.

"Here, in Cape Town."

Philip chuckled, "Close enough. I could walk there," he said, tongue in cheek while Emma hit send button.

"I'm proud of you, Philip. You never speak about your feelings about the accident, or your love for Mike, and I often wondered if you'd ever get over him. Instead, you wrote it all down in a beautiful story that keeps his memory alive. That's something."

Philip smiled, "It hasn't been easy, you know. Putting all those emotions into words was like reopening old wounds, but it also felt like a way to honour his memory and find some closure. And hey, who knew writing a romance novel would be my therapy session?"

Emma chuckled softly. "Well, it's cheaper than a therapist, that's for sure! It's more than just a story; it's a heartfelt tribute to the love you shared with Mike. You've immortalized your feelings and experiences on those pages, and that's a gift not just for you but for readers as well."

Philip nodded, grateful for Emma's understanding and support. "You know me too well, Em. I always struggle to put my feelings into words, but writing this novel allowed me to express what I couldn't say out loud. It's like Mike's presence is woven into every sentence, reminding me that love can be timeless and enduring."

Emma gave his hand a gentle squeeze. "He'll always be a part of you, Philip, and now, through your writing, a part of the world too. So, even though you might be exhausted and unsure about the future, remember that you've already achieved something remarkable."

Emma turned to her laptop and hit the send button.

"There it goes," Philip said, waving goodbye.

With the letter out of the way, Emma turned to more pressing matters. "Okay, mister. Back to business. How far have we come with next Saturday's wedding for Betty-Ann Stewart and Douw Henry?"

"Everything's organized," Philip said. "Both opted for an evening out with their friends, Douw wants a stripper, and get this, Betty Anne wants a stripper too. This seems to be a case of a final celebration of singlehood for both of them. I thought Betty-Anne would choose a less indulgent celebration because she comes from a religious family and her uncle is a Bishop."

"That's not odd. It's just plain old personal preference because they find it exciting and liberating to have this type of entertainment. We live in strange times, Philip."

"I guess we do. Do you want to stay for dinner?"

"I would love to but I have some work to do. For now, let's focus on your book becoming a bestseller...."

She left just before sunset, and Philip retired early. He reflected on the events as he settled into his bed. He couldn't deny the joy that had come from meeting Richard. It was a pleasant surprise, a bright spot in an otherwise dark world. As he lay on his bed, he replayed their conversation on the balcony. Richard's charisma had made a lasting impression; a blend of confidence and warmth. His words flowed effortlessly, drawing Philip like a gentle current. There was an authenticity to his demeanour, a genuine interest in connecting and making Philip feel at ease. His smile held a certain magnetism, captivating attention without demanding it. His gestures were fluid and inviting, creating an atmosphere of comfort and camaraderie.

As Philip reflected, he realized that Richard's charisma wasn't overpowering or flashy. Instead, it was a quiet yet powerful presence that could light up a room without stealing the spotlight. It was the kind of charisma that made you feel seen, heard, and understood – a rare quality that Philip found intriguing and captivating. With these thoughts swirling in his mind, Philip's eyelids grew heavy, and he slowly drifted into a peaceful sleep, the memory of Richard's charisma lingering like a comforting embrace.

# Chapter 3

Richard stood at the window, lost in his thoughts of how wonderful nature worked. The tide was coming in spectacularly, and the gentle sound of waves swishing off the rocks reached his ears. He leaned against the windowsill, his gaze fixed on the ocean's rhythmic dance, finding comfort in its perfectly simple orchestration. June's home always lulled him into a peaceful state of mind, a sanctuary from his busy life. Nature spoke to his soul, reminding him to slow down, to appreciate the little moments, and to find the beauty in everything that surrounded him. It was these simple moments of connection with the natural world that grounded him.

A soft knock on the door interrupted his thoughts. He tightened the robe's rope as he turned towards the sound. "Come on in," he welcomed. June entered, carrying a tray with cereal and steaming coffee.

"Good morning, young man. Enjoying the view?" Her warm voice filled the room as she placed the tray on his bedside table.

"Good morning," he greeted with a smile. "This view never gets old. It's a wonder of nature."

"Some mornings," June began, her eyes twinkling, "you can see the line where the two oceans meet."

Richard's eyes lit up with curiosity. "Really? In all the years I've lived in Cape Town, I've never seen that. Is it visible today?"

June approached the window, and he joined her, their gazes locked on the expanse before them. With a gentle motion of her hand, she directed his attention. "There," she said, her finger tracing an almost imperceptible line that seemed to divide the waters. "The 'line of demarcation.' It's where the colder waters of the Benguela Current from the south meet the warmer waters of the Agulhas Current from the north. It's quite a sight. Can you see it?"

He squinted, his focus sharpening, until the line came into clearer view. "It's incredible," he breathed, awe filling his voice. "Right here, two great forces collide."

June smiled knowingly. "Sounds like two people I know."

"Okay, I'm listening."

"You and Philip. What do you think of him?"

He hesitated, his gaze returning to the distant line in the ocean. "Honestly, besides the fact that he's a wedding planner and an author and a dish and I couldn't take my eyes off him? I think he's shy and introverted. Like something is holding him back. We didn't have enough time to connect, but the little time we did have together he seemed nervous with me around."

"He's been through a lot," June began, her voice softening. "He does tend to get nervous. Six years ago, he lost his husband in an air crash. Mike was the pilot. He doesn't speak about him at all. Hasn't mingled or even dated since. When COVID hit us, he was quite happy to go it alone, cabin fever and all."

"He lost his husband? I'm sorry to hear that."

"It shattered him. Philip was totally in love with Mike. When Mike passed on, writing became Philip's refuge. A way to keep his husband's memory alive."

Richard's expression softened. "Some wounds are too deep to share easily."

June sighed, her gaze distant. "Philip is private. Opening up after Mike's loss has been a journey. Meeting you seemed to bring him joy."

A warmth spread through Richard's chest. "He's a remarkable person."

"Absolutely. He deserves happiness after everything."

Richard nodded, his heart connecting with Philip's journey. "I hope he finds it."

"Perhaps you'll play a part in that," June mused.

As Richard looked at the line of demarcation, thoughts of connections and fate mingled in his mind. With a grateful smile, he turned to June. "Thank you for sharing."

June's smile was filled with hope. "Why don't you join us on Tuesday. Maybe the future holds something special."

Richard's smile matched hers. "I'd love to."

"Philip visits every Tuesday for lunch. You told me on the way home last night that you're flying out tomorrow to collect a newly married couple from Upington. Will you be back on Tuesday?"

"Yes. Tuesday morning around nine-thirty. I'd love to come. I have a whole two weeks school break coming up from tomorrow, so that's a plus. I have just one special lesson lined up on Wednesday for about five kids who don't get Nicholas Sparks."

"Nicholas Sparks? *He's so gettable.* His novels are excellent. But, now that you're on holiday, maybe spend a few days here."

"You're too kind, June. You don't have to..."

"I insist. It'll do the world of good for you."

"I'd like that, thank you. And I'll bring my toothbrush."

# Chapter 4

Silas Turner carefully flipped open the pages of Philip's manuscript he had printed out. His gaze fixed on the printed words, tracing each line with a hunger for the story. The office walls melted away, leaving only the vivid scenes of the story playing in his mind. As he flipped the pages, the characters leapt off the paper, their struggles and triumphs igniting a fire within him and time slipped through his fingers as he delved deeper into the narrative. His heart hammered against his chest, the echoes of the story's emotions reverberating within him. After hours spent engrossed in the narrative, he reluctantly closed the manuscript. Leaving the cocoon of his office, he stepped out into the fading sunlight, the echo of Philip's words accompanying him on his journey home.

At home he sank into the plush armchair in his cozy reading nook, his fingers eagerly tracing the page where he had left off. The soft lamplight spilled a warm embrace across the room, tendrils of golden glow stretching to chase away the shadows, leaving them to dance playfully on the walls. As he read on, a magnetic pull seemed to draw him deeper into the manuscript's world, every word wrapping around his heart.

As he turned the pages, the author's artistry unfurled like a blossoming flower, each petal revealing a new layer of brilliance. His breath caught in his throat, and a sense of wonder tightened his grip on the pages. With each revelation, an insatiable hunger grew within him, urging him to devour more. He had read countless manuscripts as a publisher, and more often than not, he was disappointed by the lacklustre offerings on his desk.

However, when he delved into Philip Mitchell's manuscript, it was as if he had stepped into a crisp breeze after a long stifling day. The prose danced with vitality, and the characters breathed with life, rekindling his hope for exceptional storytelling.

The narrative unfolded around an event planner who, in the wake of a soul-shattering disclosure of his husband's betrayal, found himself adrift in a sea of disillusionment. Seeking refuge from the storm of emotions, he left behind the icy grip of Johannesburg, and moved to Cape Town. He did not expect to meet Michael Livingstone.

What could be more intriguing than falling in love with an aviator? Michael embodied the exhilarating freedom of flight, a personification of the age-old human desire to defy gravity and touch the heavens. His world was one of soaring aspirations and wide-open horizons, where the sky is not a limit but a canvas of endless possibilities.

They learned that love, much like flight, required trust, vulnerability, and the willingness to venture into the unknown. However, this was not just a romance, it was also a about Mike's death.

Each unexpected bend was a hook that dug into Silas's curiosity, leaving him teetering on the edge of his seat. The layers of the narrative, like fine layers of paint on an exquisite canvas, had been meticulously thought out, each detail contributing to the skill of storytelling. Characters became companions, their vibrant personalities leaping off the page. Their emotions were complex, an intricate dance of joy and sorrow that tugged at Silas's heartstrings, urging him to feel what they felt.

An unbidden smile found its way to Silas's lips. In this sea of manuscripts that drifted across his desk, he had unearthed a gem that shone brighter than all the rest. It was a treasure trove of imagination, a testament to Philip's artistry and dedication.

As Silas closed the manuscript, a sense of gratitude washed over him. He had been granted a rare glimpse into a world that had the power to both transport and transform. With the manuscript resting in his hands, he knew that he had embarked on a journey that was destined to leave an indelible mark on his literary soul.

The door swung open with a flourish, and Jack Bolding strode into Silas's study, his luggage rolling behind him. His shoulders were squared, each step an air of confidence. 'Home sweet home.'

Jack exuded a charm that had drawn Silas to him fifteen years ago. Sleek blond hair framed Jack's face, every strand perfectly coaxed into place. His striking features, chiselled jaw, and eyes that held a glint of mischief enhanced the magnetic allure that had once drawn Silas to him.

Silas's gaze flickered briefly over Jack's confident facade, memories of past encounters coloured his perception. He knew all too well that appearances could be deceiving, that behind Jack's charming smile often lay motives hidden like shadows in plain sight. Silas's mind flickered back to conversations, subtle twists of words that had played out like carefully orchestrated performances. He remembered the moments when Jack had adeptly steered situations to his favour, leaving others unsuspecting, their trust unshaken.

"What have you been up to, my love?" Jack inquired.

Silas gazed up at him, and with a hesitant smile, pushed the manuscript across the table. "This is something special. We have another winner," Silas said. "I thought of you when I read it. It gave me goose bumps, in the best way possible."

Jack read the name of the author out loud. "Philip Mitchell?"

"His bio says that he's a Wedding Planner and he's self-published several books."

'I'll take a look tonight. But first I need to shower. Damn! What a day."

"Tell me some good news," Silas said.

"Chrome Books and Nova Books signed with us; the first three months are on a consignment basis only. They're taking our complete backlist with our promise that after six months they have a right to rotate unsold stock."

"That's great! I guess you deserve that shower. Your food is in the microwave by the way."

"Not hungry. Had a huge lunch with the sales manager at Nova," Jack said. Taking the manuscript with him, he headed towards their bedroom, where he took a refreshing shower. He emerged from the bathroom, and called out to Silas, his voice a gentle summons to join him in bed.

Silas, however, had immersed himself in a world of manuscripts from other writers, a sea of words from a slush-pile that demanded his attention. His responsibilities urged him to stay in his study and complete the task at hand. With a soft apology, he declined Jack's invitation, choosing instead to remain immersed in his work.

***

As Jack settled into the softness of the pillow, the exhaustion that engulfed him quickly claimed his senses and he surrendered to sleep, only to awaken at 2:30 am.

A craving for water had nudged him awake, but he made a cup of coffee instead. With the steaming cup cradled in his hands, Jack returned to the comfort of their bed, drawing the manuscript close.

He delved into Philip's novel and was instantly captivated by the author's mastery. Time slipped away, unnoticed, as Jack journeyed through the pages, consumed by the world created by Philip's pen, leaving him spellbound and yearning for more.

At the first rays of dawn, Jack reluctantly tore his gaze away from the pages. He slammed the manuscript shut and stepped out onto the balcony and watched as Cape Town awakened. Tall buildings reached towards the heavens, their silhouettes casting long shadows in the early morning light. The bustling streets below came alive, each corner holding its own stories and secrets.

At that moment, Jack realised the magnitude of what he had just read. The work had the potential to become a prize-winning book, destined to leave an indelible mark on the literary world. With a burning desire to share his thoughts, he retreated from the balcony and prepared breakfast.

A half hour later, Silas joined him at the table.

"I read the manuscript," Jack exclaimed.

"You did? All of it?" he asked, anticipation bubbling within him.

"I have no words. It's pure gold. It's going to need some editing, but not too much," he said. "Just one thing nags at me — will Mitchell deliver more masterpieces like this?"

Silas leaned back in his chair, pondering Jack's question. "A three-book contract could lead to even greater achievements. I don't believe he's a one-hit wonder. And even if he is, so what? His namesake, Margaret Mitchell, was a one-book wonder with 'Gone with the Wind' in 1936, and look at the monumental success she achieved."

"Do you think he's related to her?"

Silas furrowed his brow. "An interesting thought. I'll have to ask him."

***

On Monday evening, Philip sat in his cluttered study. The air conditioning hummed softly in the background. Papers and notebooks scattered all over his desk. Anxiously, he refreshed his email inbox. He looked at the screen and saw the name Bolt Publishing pop up. His heart raced with excitement as he eagerly clicked on the email and read it:

*From: Silas Turner (silas.turner@Boltpublishing.com)*

*To: Philip Mitchell (Philip.mitchell@gmail.com)*

*Dear Mr. Mitchell,*

*Thank you for reaching out to Bolt Publishing with your query. I must say, the first three chapters of "Final Flight" caught my attention from the very first page. Your storytelling ability and captivating characters have left me wanting more.*

*I am writing to express my keen interest in reading the full manuscript of 'Final Flight'. The premise and themes explored in your novel align perfectly with our publishing vision at Bolt and we believe your work has the potential to resonate with our readers and make a significant impact in the romance genre.*

*If you are amenable, I would be delighted to review the complete manuscript at your earliest convenience. Rest assured it will receive my utmost attention and consideration.*

*I look forward to delving further into your work and discovering the depths of the story you have crafted.*

*Warm regards,*

*Silas Turner*

*Editor and CEO*

Bolt Publishing

A wide smile transformed his face into a reflection of inner delight. He could hardly contain his elation, and his fingers trembled with anticipation while he drafted a quick reply and attached the manuscript.

*Subject: Full Manuscript Attached!*

*Dear Mr. Turner,*

*I hope this email finds you well. First and foremost, I want to express my sincere gratitude for your interest in "Final Flight" and your request to see the full manuscript. I cannot adequately put into words the excitement and joy I felt upon reading your email. Your belief in my story is incredibly validating and fills me with renewed determination.*

*Without further ado, I have attached the complete manuscript of "Final Flight" to this email. I have meticulously poured my heart and soul into every word. I hope it delivers on the promise and potential it holds.*

*I want to take this opportunity to thank you for considering my work. It is an honour to have the chance to work with Bolt Publishing. Your dedication to nurturing talented authors is truly inspiring, and I am thrilled to have the opportunity to potentially join your esteemed list of authors.*

*Please feel free to reach out if you have any questions or require any further information. I eagerly await your feedback and the possibility of taking the next steps toward publication.*

*With heartfelt appreciation,*

*Philip Mitchell*

Eager to share the news, he punched in Emma's number. As the phone rang, he paced back and forth, the carpet soft beneath his feet.

"Hello?" Emma's voice rang out.

"Emma, guess what?"

"Philip? You sound like you've just won the lottery," she replied.

"Silas Turner at Bolt Publishing wants to see the full manuscript!" Philip's words tumbled out in a rush.

A brief pause. An eruption of joyous laughter. Philip joined in, the sound of their elation echoing through his cellphone.

"Wow! That was quick!" Emma said. "We only sent it yesterday. We did it! I knew your story would captivate them. Have you sent the full manuscript?"

"You know how it is. I really had to think twice before hitting the send button. I mean, what if he finds something wrong with it? Something I didn't see?"

"Please tell me you sent it."

"Yes, a few minutes ago."

Emma sighed with relief. "Now, you just need to wait."

"Waiting is always the worst part." Philip tapped his fingers nervously on the kitchen counter.

"What's wrong? Why are you tapping? I can hear it." Emma said.

"I'm trying to summon the magical powers of speedy publishing by tapping my fingers. You know, like a romance-themed rain dance."

Emma laughed. "Well, keep tapping, and maybe they'll publish it in record time."

"If they do accept my book, we are going to celebrate, girl!"

"Deal! We'll celebrate like there's no tomorrow."

"Seriously though, what if they do accept it for publication? What if it becomes an out-of-control international bestseller, like Rowling or Tolkien's work?"

"Firstly, let's get the genre right. Those are fantasy. Yours is romance, so let's compare it to Steel or Sparks instead. Just think, you'll never need to work again. On second thoughts that's highly unlikely because I need you. So, I'll see you at the office later?"

"I'll be there."

# Chapter 5

On Tuesday morning Philip spilled his breakfast cereal when his phone rang. It displaying an unknown number. "If this is a sales pitch, I'm not interested," he said.

"It's Silas Turner from Bolt Publishing."

Philip's grip loosened around the mop handle, and it clanged onto the tiled floor. "Mr. Turner?" he stammered, his heart pounding in his chest.

"Yes, but please call me Silas."

"I guess you hated the rest of my manuscript?" Philip's voice quivered.

Silas chuckled. "You should give yourself more credit, Mr. Mitchell. I didn't hate it, I loved it."

Philip's legs weakened, and he had to find a seat to steady himself. "You did?" he said, struggling to grasp the magnitude of Silas's words.

"Your manuscript is everything I've been looking for and more. I'd like to offer you an advance on a three-book contract."

Philip's jaw dropped, speechless for a moment. "An advance? A three-book contract?"

Silas continued, "Plus 10% royalties on all three books."

Philip's mind raced, his disbelief slowly transforming into awe. "You're... you're not serious, surely."

Silas laughed, "I'm very serious. I need to see you at my office this morning to finalise the contract. Once it's signed, we'll pay you the advance immediately."

"I... I don't know what to say. Are you sure about this?"

Silas reassured him, his voice brimming with confidence. "Does nine this morning suit you? I don't mind if you're late. This must seem sudden to you."

Philip's eyes welled up with tears of joy. "Yes, absolutely. Nine it is. Thank you."

"Thank yourself, Philip. You're a talented writer, and we're thrilled you reached out to us. Get ready for an incredible journey."

As they concluded the call, Philip sat in stunned silence while this life-changing news sunk in. He took a deep breath, trying to calm his racing heart. With trembling fingers he dialled Emma's number.

"Morning, I'm getting ready for work. What's up?"

"They're offering me one and a half million rand per book for three books," Philip blurted out, unable to contain his excitement.

"What?"

"Silas Turner, from Bolt Publishing, just called. He offered me a three-book contract, and an advance of one and a half million rand per book and 10% royalties on all three books," he explained.

Emma let out a shriek so loud Philip had to hold the phone away from his ear. He imagined her jumping around with joy. "Where are you?" she finally asked.

"At home but not for long, I have to be at Bolt Publishing in an hour and a half."

"Wow! They don't mess around, do they?"

Philip smiled, "Girl, I don't care. I'm ready to tackle the world."

# Chapter 6

No sooner had Silas ended the call to Philip than he clicked open an email from Neil Ramsay, author of their current bestseller and stared at the computer screen in disbelief, his heart sinking with each word. The author had taken ill and would be unable to fulfil his role as the facilitator. Panic gripped Silas's chest as he realised the implications of this unforeseen predicament.

The workshop, fully booked, now hung in the balance. Silas had a monumental task ahead of him. With just one week until the workshop commenced, finding a suitable replacement was an insurmountable challenge.

His mind raced, desperately searching for a solution. He paced back and forth; his usually composed demeanour now shattered. The success of the workshop was crucial, not only for the attendees but also for the reputation of Bolt Publishing.

He furiously sent out emails and made frantic phone calls, reaching out to every author and literary figure he could think of, but each had prior arrangements.

At eight on the dot, Jack entered the room carrying two cups of steaming coffee in his hands. Clad in a sleek black suit, crisp white shirt, and a matching black tie, he immediately noticed the distress etched across Silas's face. Setting the cup down, he said, "What's up? You look as if the world has ended."

Silas mumbled. "I just received an email from Neil Ramsay."

"And?"

"He's fallen ill. He won't be available for the workshop."

"Not good. We've organised everything for him, including flight tickets and hotel expenses. What do we do now?"

Silas took a moment to gather his thoughts. "First, we need to send him a bouquet of flowers and cancel his flight," he began. "Secondly, I have to find a replacement speaker for the workshop. And thirdly, we need to get the contract prepped for Philip Mitchell."

"Did you find out if he's related to Margaret Mitchell? It could be a huge marketing drive," Jack asked.

"Damn! I forgot. He's coming in at nine and I'll ask him. What about you? You look like you're on your way to a funeral," Silas said.

"I have an appointment with Seamus O'Leary, an Irish film producer. He wants to discuss Ramsay's bestseller and potentially turn it into a film."

"I remember you saying something about that in our last meeting. I had no idea you'd arranged it so soon," Silas said, surprised.

"The sooner the better. It will be our first book-to-movie deal. I don't want to stuff it up," he gulped the last of the coffee and headed for the door. "See you later."

"No kiss today?"

Jack turned at the door and blew him a kiss as Silas pressed his secretary's number into his phone.

***

The anticipation of Philip's first meeting with a mainstream publisher bubbled under the surface, threatening to burst with every passing moment. Besides Emma, there was only one person who could truly appreciate the significance of this moment — the person who had instilled in him a love for words and storytelling — his mother, a seasoned, albeit retired, journalist.

"Hi, Mom," he greeted.

"Philip! You're still coming, aren't you," June's voice filled the line, brimming with affection.

Philip wasted no time in sharing his exhilarating news. "I have incredible news for you. Bolt Publishing has offered me a publishing deal!"

"Oh, darling, what wonderful news! Tell me all about it."

Philip settled into a chair, recounting every detail of his upcoming meeting. He described the publisher's interest in his novel, the potential for his work to reach a wider audience, and the possibilities ahead.

June's journalist background kicked in as she asked insightful questions and offered words of encouragement. She understood the significance of this milestone in Philip's writing journey and shared in his enthusiasm. "I'm so proud of you, Philip," she said, her voice filled with pride and maternal love. "This is just the beginning for you. Keep chasing your dreams, and remember, I'm always here to support you."

As Philip basked in the warmth of his mother's words, he felt a surge of gratitude for having someone so wise and knowledgeable in his corner. He was not alone on this creative path; both June and Emma believed in him and understood the intricacies of the writing world.

A sense of relief washed over him. "Thank you, Mom."

"I'll see you for lunch?"

"I have a nine-o-clock appointment with the publishers and I'll probably be running late, but I'll be there."

"Wonderful. I'll see you later. Oh, and Richard will be joining us, you remember Richard, from Barbara's wedding?" she said.

"How could I forget?"

"He can't stop talking about you. Loves the idea that you're an author and piano player."

"I wanted to give him my cell number but he never said goodbye at the wedding."

"Well, make sure to give it to him when you see him later."

"I won't forget. I have to run, Mom. Have a great day and give my love to Dad."

# Chapter 7

The moment Philip crossed the threshold into the sleek boardroom of Bolt Publishing, a vibrant charge filled the air, sending a tingle up his spine. Voices hummed with excitement, and the room crackled with an energy that danced along his nerves.

Philip's gaze was drawn irresistibly to Silas, who stood in the centre of the room, a beacon of determination. Every movement Silas made and his every word resonated with a deep sense of purpose. Charisma oozed from him, captivating Philip's attention and leaving no doubt about the ambition that fuelled him.

"First off, I must say I'm impressed. Your writing style is... unique." Silas said, gesturing towards a seat.

"Thank you," Philip said, smiling.

"It's the way you explore complex themes. That's what I look for in a writer. A fresh perspective."

"Thank you."

"Ready for this?" Silas said.

"As ready as ever."

He handed Philip a copy of the contract. "First and foremost, we have the advance payment. It's an upfront sum we provide as an initial investment in your book. A gesture of faith and commitment from Bolt Publishing. You'll get one and a half million rand the moment you sign the contract. When you give us the second book, you'll get an amount reflecting your sales position. It might be more; it might be less. In fact, Mary, my secretary, is waiting for your banking details as we speak."

"Excuse me if I seem over-excited, but how does the advance payment work exactly? Is it deducted from future earnings?"

"No. The advance payment is separate from your future earnings. It's an upfront sum for you to keep. It's our way of supporting you financially and allowing you to focus on your writing without immediate financial concerns."

Philip's face lit up with gratitude and a lump formed in his throat. "You have no idea how much I appreciate it."

"Your Bio says you're a wedding planner."

"Yes, I plan weddings and events with my partner, Emma."

"Tiring work. You seem nervous."

"I am," Philip chuckled.

"Don't be. This is all to your advantage. According to our contract, you'll receive 10% of the net sales for each copy of your book sold based on the net sales generated by the book, paid out every three months."

Philip leaned forward. "So, for every book sold, I'll earn a percentage of the net sales, not gross revenue?"

"Remember, as a publishing house we have overheads. We hire professional editors and proof-readers to polish the manuscript to make it error-free. Their expertise comes at a cost, but it's essential to ensure the quality of the book. We also invest in skilled designers to create visually appealing and appropriate covers to catch the readers' attention. Moving on, we have printing and production costs. This includes the actual printing of physical copies, as well as the binding, paper, and other materials required. These costs vary based on the book's format and volume of copies."

Philip leaned in, absorbing the information. "How many units will you print?"

"First print run will be ten thousand. And for us to sell them we will need extensive marketing and promotion, advertising, online campaigns, book launch events, and travel for you and us to increase the book's visibility to reach its target audience. We work with distributors and handle logistics, storage, and transportation to get the books to bookstores, online retailers, and libraries."

Philip contemplated the logistics involved. "It sounds complex."

Silas nodded, appreciating Philip's understanding. "It can be quite involved, but it's a necessary part of the publishing process. There are other expenses like salaries for employees, software licences, legal fees, and other general overheads."

Philip's eyes widened. "I had no idea it was this involved. And it's all paid for from the money my book makes? In essence, *I am* paying for the book to be published."

Silas chuckled, "I understand it may seem like a rip off, but if your book flops, we carry the expense. If your book is a success, it's all worth it and we make a profit too."

Philip's excitement grew, but he had another question on his mind. "What about copyright ownership?"

Silas leaned back. "You own the copyright. However, once you sign on the dotted line, you give Bolt exclusive rights to publish and distribute your work worldwide."

"Can I ask when it will be published?"

"It can take anything from three months to a year."

"A year?"

"Give or take, yes. But with this manuscript I'm looking at maybe three months before it hits the shelves."

"Awesome."

"Now, let's discuss marketing and promotion. The contract outlines the strategies Bolt Publishing will undertake to maximise the book's visibility and reach. We'll plan book launches, publicity campaigns, and online marketing efforts to give your book the exposure it deserves. You'll need to travel when required, locally and overseas. Are you available?"

Philip's eyes widened. "I'm available. Except, I have a fear of flying."

"There's going to be a whole lot of flying. I can understand your fear from what you have written. We believe in your book, and we'll do everything we can to ensure its success, even if it means getting some help for you. Transparency is key in our partnership. One last question."

Philip smiled, "Shoot."

"Are you in?"

"A hundred percent I'm in."

Silas retrieved a gold pen from his shirt pocket. He called in Mary and another staff member to serve as witnesses to the signing. The gold pen gleamed in Silas's hand as he handed it to Philip.

"First fill in this page with your banking details, and then sign at the bottom of each page," Silas said. After the signing, the witnesses left the office, leaving Silas and Philip alone.

"Welcome to your new home, Philip," Silas shook Philip's hand.

"I'm glad to be here."

"You deserve every bit of success, and I have no doubt you'll make the most of this opportunity."

A long silence followed as Silas gazed at Philip, taking in his face and hands as though he'd never see them again.

Philip asked, "What?"

Silas smiled, "I was just thinking if your book would have been accepted elsewhere."

"Bolt is the only place I sent it to."

Silas checked the time. "So no other publisher knows about this. That's a plus. I have another appointment in fifteen minutes. I'll walk you out." He gestured towards the office door, and led the way with Philip following closely behind towards the elevator.

The elevator doors opened and, just as Silas thought their conversation had come to a close, he couldn't resist asking one final question, his curiosity getting the better of him. He reached out, gently touching Philip's arm. "Can I ask, are you related to Margaret Mitchell?"

"Actually, yes. She was my great-great-great grandmother's aunt on my father's side."

"Well then, you have some damned big shoes to fill."

# Chapter 8

Sitting at the dining table, June was excited, like when one shakes a soda and it fizzes up. "Your publishing deal is amazing! Your book will be in stores soon. I'm really proud of you."

Philip's face lit up. "It's like my dream came true, Mom. I can't believe it. It's even better than what I imagined."

"You were meant to be a super famous writer, just like your great grand aunt. I can already see myself going to a store, pointing and saying, 'That's my son's book!'"

Their attention pivoted as Richard entered with a friendly smile.

"Richard!" Philip said. "It's really nice to see you again."

Richard's smile revealed a little dent in his cheek. "Likewise, Philip. Thanks for inviting me, June," he said.

"My pleasure. Sit down and grab yourself a glass of wine. There's lasagne, Philip's favourite meal and a Greek salad with feta cheese."

"Looks yum. Thanks."

While Richard poured himself a glass of red, June held her glass up and announced, "To my son and his success as an author. Don't forget you have a mother."

Richard said, "Your mom told me your manuscript was accepted by Bolt. Congratulations. I guess you won't need me as a Beta now."

"You talk as if there's only one book in me. I have tons more."

June interrupted, "Maybe Richard can help you edit the next one?"

"Edit? I don't understand," Philip said.

"I'm a member of the South African Editors Forum," Richard said.

"I... I'm confused now. You said you teach."

"I also edit in my spare time. There's something magical about books, isn't there?"

Philip nodded. "It's a warm place to escape. Do you also write?"

"I do. My motivation comes from poetry and the epics."

Philip's eyes lit up with curiosity. "Poetry and epics? Fascinating. What kind of stories do you write?"

"Tales of epic adventures, where heroes face unimaginable challenges and embark on journeys to test their courage and strength. The power of words in poetry has always mesmerized me, and I try to infuse the same magic into my storytelling."

"It takes a special talent to weave poetry and epic storytelling together."

Richard chuckled modestly. "I'm still finding my voice as a writer, but it's a journey I'm passionate about. It's a beautiful art form."

"I couldn't agree more," Philip said.

"What about planning weddings?" Richard asked. "Are you still going to organise them?"

Philip chuckled, "It may seem worlds apart from writing, but there's a certain magic in bringing people's dreams to life and orchestrating a wedding. Every wedding holds its own special charm, its own story. I have the privilege of helping couples craft unforgettable memories to cherish for a lifetime."

June had been silent throughout the conversation and, satisfied they had made a connection, she stood up and said, "Why don't you two go for a walk while I clear the table? I hope you boys enjoyed the food."

Philip stood up and hugged her. "Loved it, thanks Mom."

As they walked along the pathway leading down to the ocean, Richard said, "I love it here. The air is fresh and crisp the whole year round."

"As a kid I'd take long hikes up to the point," Philip remembered. "Sometimes camp out the whole weekend, by myself, no one else around. I had a whole lot of thinking to do. Had many pow-wows with God here."

"Over what?"

"Lots of things. I wanted to know if the world was round or flat, did we really land on the moon or was it myth? I asked Him what the meaning of life is. I once questioned whether being gay was right because it seemed like everything was so right for straight people," Philip reflected. "But one day, it hit me. There's no wrong or right when it comes to love and identity. If it feels right for you, it must be right. The realisation allowed me to accept myself as someone who mattered, and the opinions of everyone else no longer held the same weight."

Richard listened attentively. "How did your parents react to you coming out?" he asked, kicking a stone from beneath his feet.

"There were tears and hugs when I told them. I'll never forget the weekend after I told them. It was my nineteenth birthday on the Saturday, and my dad took me aside. He said they didn't buy me a gift but wanted to take me out for supper. We ended up at a Chinese restaurant and afterwards took a leisurely walk down the street, doing some window shopping. Suddenly, my dad stopped in front of a place called Sides. I had never heard of it before. There were two bouncers at the door, and my dad showed them three tickets. They let us in. Once we stepped inside, I looked around and realised it was a gay place. We drank, we danced, and I had the best time of my life. I knew then, without a doubt, my parents accepted and loved me unconditionally. They are just perfect. How about you? How did your parents react?"

"I can relate to having someone who's been an inspiration in my life. My parents passed away in a car accident, and my Aunt Flora raised me. She was extraordinary. She put me through college without expecting anything in return, and her unwavering support made all the difference. The day I told her I was gay she laughed and said, 'Well, I hate to tell you and I hope you're not disappointed, but I'm straight. You know, heterosexual.' We laughed and popped a bottle of champers to celebrate our coming out."

"I'd love to meet her," Philip said.

"She passed away three years ago."

"I'm so sorry. You must miss her."

"I miss her every day," he replied, his voice low and melancholy. "She was my rock, my guiding light."

"It sounds like she cared deeply for you."

"She did. Before she passed, she made me promise to find a love that would last a lifetime, someone who would never leave me feeling lonely. It's why I've chosen to live alone all this time, waiting for the perfect man. But sometimes, I wonder if finding such a love is even possible. Is it normal to hold out for something so extraordinary?"

"People fall in love all the time. Mostly just to be with someone," Philip said. "They think it's true love but really, it's just someone they happen to love at the time, like I love my jeans, or my shoes, or the house I live in. I think true love is different, it's so difficult to achieve because it's so elusive and not just about physical attraction. It goes much deeper."

"I like your wisdom," Richard said, smiling. "It's like your soul has been places."

"I believe in true love."

Richard's eyes bore into Philip's with intensity. "I do too. And, talking about love, I would really love for you to join me for dinner tonight."

Philip's heart skipped a beat as he took Richard's hand, feeling the warmth and tenderness in the touch. "I won't say no."

Philip nodded, his gaze locked with Richard's. "Today has been incredible, and I've enjoyed our time together." But, inside, he wanted Richard to hold him. It grew like a flickering flame, its warmth spreading through his veins, yearning for intimacy, for the tenderness of a lover's touch.

A genuine smile spread across Richard's face. "I did too, Philip Mitchell."

They made their way back to the house. June, brimming with curiosity and excitement, couldn't contain her enthusiasm and prodded them for details about their walk. But the two men exchanged smiles, as if sharing a secret.

"It was kind of... spiritual, Mom," Philip finally replied, trying to find a diplomatic way to describe their experience. "But hey, at least he invited me for dinner tonight."

"Perfect!" June exclaimed, her eyes sparkling with anticipation. "There's this charming little restaurant right here at Cape Point, Mandy's. I'll make a booking right away. And, Philip, I've prepared your room for tonight. Richard gets the spare room." June couldn't resist a playful jab at her son. "My son never sleeps over as if we have some kind of rabid disease."

Philip rolled his eyes, accustomed to his mother's teasing. "Maybe your son is too busy with his own life?"

June chuckled, "True, true. Let me make the booking at Mandy's."

***

The soft lighting in Mandy's Restaurant created an intimate ambiance and a gentle melody played in the background. They found their table and Richard pulled out a chair out for Philip.

As they settled into their seats, Richard said, "I met your parents at this restaurant."

"You did?"

"It was stupid thing. I got up from my chair to use the men's room and your parents were seated at the table behind us. Your mom got up at the same time and the waiter arrived just as I stood up. I didn't see the waiter and, boom, all the drinks for their table went tumbling to the floor. I spoiled your mom's dress. We've been friends ever since."

"My mom is a beautiful person inside out. She's always been supportive. Never sees the bad in people."

"She is amazing, but so is your dad."

Philip chuckled, his heart warm with affection as he thought of his dad. "My dad is pretty amazing. Quiet. Observes. Loves fishing."

"So, tell me about planning weddings."

"It's hard work. Each wedding is unique, and it's all about creating a day that reflects the couple's love story and personalities. From selecting the perfect venue to designing the floral arrangements. I coordinate every little detail."

"It sounds like a lot of work."

"It definitely is," Philip said with a smile. "But, it's also rewarding. Seeing the joy on the couple's faces when they walk down the aisle, knowing I had a hand in creating something special, is a feeling out of this world. But there are also moments of stress and chaos, like dealing with last-minute changes or unexpected challenges. But, it's all worth it to see two people start their journey together."

"It sounds like you have a passion for bringing love and happiness to people's lives."

"Love is such a powerful force, and every wedding is like a small piece of magic."

Their conversation flowed effortlessly; the intimacy of the restaurant matched the growing connection between them. They shared stories, dreams, and laughter, it became clear they were kindred spirits, drawn together by a shared appreciation for love, literature, and the wonders of the world.

"I know we spoke about true love earlier today, but have you ever been deeply in love, Richard?"

A wistful expression crossed Richard's face as memories flooded back. He took a sip of wine before responding. "His name was Joseph. Five years older than me. He taught me so much about life, about love, and about embracing every moment. We met at a teacher's conference and went home the very first night. He moved in with me after six months and everything was going just fine, then his dad fell ill and he wanted to be with him. He moved out and I haven't seen him since. He contacted me three months later. Told me he had found someone new and would never forget me."

Philip listened attentively, his heart going out to Richard as he shared his bittersweet memories of Joseph. The wistful expression on Richard's face spoke volumes.

"I'm sorry," Philip said softly, reaching out to gently touch Richard's hand. "It must have been incredibly difficult to go through such a challenging time during the pandemic."

Richard nodded, a mix of sadness and fondness in his eyes. "Losing him was one of the hardest things I've ever experienced. We had this connection that defied all odds, but sometimes life takes unexpected turns. Still, I don't think it was true love."

"Do you miss him?"

"I think about him now and then, and part of me will always love him. But I also know life goes on, and we find a way to move forward, even if it feels impossible at times. How about you?"

"I've only ever known one man."

"Your mom told me," Richard said. "You must have gone through hell. If you don't want to speak about it, I understand."

"Mike was the most amazing man. A good man. Someone to rely on, to trust, to lean on. He always rooted for the underdog. He was just perfect in every way."

"How did you meet him?" Richard asked.

Philip took a deep breath. "It all started when I was involved with someone who turned out to be a bit wild and obsessed with sex. One day, I walked in on him having sex with another guy."

Richard's eyebrows shot up in surprise, but he kept listening, intrigued by the unfolding tale.

"We broke up and I decided to come to Cape Town to visit mom, so I booked a flight through Mike's company."

Philip's eyes softened with memories as he continued. "Mike and I hit it off right away. We had an instant connection, and he became a crucial part of my life. Mike had just bought the cottage at Llandudno and he invited me to move in with him. At first I was doubtful, but I was prepared to give it a go. Our home was filled with love and laughter."

"It sounds like you guys had a special bond."

"I fell in love with him from the moment I saw him, and he felt the same way. But our journey wasn't without its ups and downs. We faced challenges, but we fought through them, and for four incredible years we were together."

The air grew heavy with unspoken sorrow as Richard asked the inevitable question, his voice gentle, "What happened?"

A flicker of pain crossed Philip's face, and he replied quietly, "He passed away in a plane crash."

Richard's heart sank, realising the depth of loss Philip had experienced. He reached out and placed a comforting hand on Philip's, offering silent support.

"I'm so sorry," he whispered.

"It's what my book is about. I vowed never to fall in love with a pilot again. In fact, I vowed never to fall in love with anyone else."

Richard raised an eyebrow, intrigued and curious about Philip's decision. "Never again?"

Philip nodded; his gaze fixed on a distant point as if he were reliving moments from his past. "Mike was my anchor, my partner, and my best friend. Losing him... it shattered me."

"I can't even begin to imagine what you went through."

Philip continued, his tone introspective. "I poured all my emotions into writing, into creating a world where I could hold onto his memory. The book has become a tribute, a way to keep him alive."

"And meeting me, does it stir up those feelings?"

Philip's eyes met Richard's, and for a moment, the air felt charged with unspoken emotions. "You're different," he smiled. "You make me question the promises I made to myself."

Richard's touch on Philip's hand tightened. "Sometimes, life has a way of leading us down unexpected paths. It's okay to reconsider, to open your heart again."

"You have a way of making things seem a little less daunting," Philip said, smiling.

"That's the power of genuine connection," Richard said, a sincere warmth in his eyes.

The night seemed to shimmer through the chemistry they shared. And then, suddenly, the rhythm of their conversation wavered, notes of silence threaded through their words. Philip noticed the quiet settling over Richard like a veil of mist rolling in from the ocean. It was as if the evening breeze carried a change, a quiet introspection replacing the earlier cadence of excitement.

"You're suddenly quiet," Philip said.

"I guess it's because the evening is coming to an end and I don't want it to."

"I feel the same way."

***

After dinner, they strolled along the winding path leading up to the point. As they walked, the call of a distant whale caught their attention.

"Listen. Isn't that crazy beautiful?" Richard said.

"It never ceases to amaze me. Tell me about your other romances."

Richard smiled, his eyes distant as he delved into the chapters of his love life. "Well, none of my romances can quite compare to yours. You know about Joseph, but there was this one guy who truly swept me off my feet. His name was Cayden, an American I met at a gay bar. I was a student teacher at the time and he was in South Africa for a documentary about Penguins," Richard continued. "From the moment we met, there was an instant connection. We clicked right away, and our time together was nothing short of magical. But, you see, there was a problem. Joel's visa had an expiration date — just twelve months. Afterwards, he would have to return to the USA. Aware of this, we decided to make the most of our time together, cherishing every moment. When he returned to the USA, he promised to work towards bringing me there. We had hopes and dreams of being together, building a life. However, as time went on, we lost contact, and I never saw or heard from him again. In fact, when Cayden left me, it was the last time I had sex with anyone. That was four years ago."

"You're not serious."

"It's been so long I've forgotten what it's like or even what to do," Richard said, laughing.

"I'm two years ahead of you. It's been six years for me."

"So, there hasn't been anyone else in your life since Mike passed?"

Philip chuckled, shaking his head. "No one."

Richard raised his hand in a tight fist, his voice filled with exuberance. "Here's to us, Philip and Richard!"

Philip joined in, his own voice carrying over the roaring ocean, "To us! The Cape Town virgins. Virgin Richard and Virgin Philip."

They laughed out loud and walked up the winding road to the house. Philip placed a comforting hand on Richard's shoulder, "I had a great time tonight."

"I did too. If you want to share a bed, the invite is open," Richard said, sheepishly.

"I think maybe some other time. My parents house and so on."

"I'll keep you to your word."

Stopping outside the door to Richard's room, they paused, staring longingly into each other's eyes. Eventually Richard said, "Are you sure you won't come in?"

"I'm sure. Goodnight, Richard."

"Goodnight, Philip."

# Chapter 9

Philip's eyes fluttered open, anticipation coursing through his veins before the first rays of dawn even kissed the horizon. With a surge of energy, he sprang out of bed and headed for the shower. The steam wrapped around him, awakening every sense. Out of curiosity he checked his bank balance. His fingers danced on the screen of his phone, accessing the gateway to his bank account. His balance had changed and suddenly he was wealthier than he had ever been. A triumphant cry escaped his lips, echoing through the confined space and the world outside responded, resonating with his exhilaration.

He was a millionaire. A culmination of talent, dedication, and unwavering belief in his craft had manifested into this extraordinary moment.

Yet, even in the midst of his newfound wealth, his heart remained tethered to the future. The success of a single book was just the beginning. As he checked his bank account, a message came through from Silas.

*Contact me urgently.*

His heart pounded as he called Silas.

"I received your message. Sorry, I was occupied with my phone. How are you?" Philip asked.

"Honestly, not so fine," Silas said.

"What's happening?"

"I've received some bad news about one of our writers. He's ill and can't fulfil his obligations right now. Seems to be Covid symptoms."

"I thought Covid was all done and dusted," Philip said.

"It's still around. This author is the host and convener of our new writer's workshop and we stand to lose a lot of money if he doesn't show. His prognosis isn't good."

"How about hiring a replacement?" Philip said.

"That's the reason I'm calling. Can you help out? We'll pay you a handsome fee to present the course. Your own course. Do you think you can dig deep and help us?"

"Are you sure about this?"

"I'm sure. The course is fully booked and everyone has paid. If I don't find someone today, the refund logistics will be a nightmare."

"You want me to deliver a series of workshops?"

"Yes, starting tomorrow."

"Tomorrow! That doesn't give me much time. I wouldn't know where to start?"

"You can write. Start there. We have a lot of work ahead of us. Today and tomorrow you'll be exhausted but don't worry, I'll be here working with you. This is urgent."

"Can I at least think about this?"

"I need your answer before midday. We can't waste time."

"I'll give it my best, Silas. I guess If it doesn't work out you can always get someone else."

"No one else writes like you."

***

Richard and June were already at the breakfast table on the patio when Philip joined them.

"Hey, mister. Did you sleep well?" Richard asked.

Philip smiled and pulled his hand through his hair. "I did, and you?"

"My beds are the most comfortable in the world," June said, dishing out scrambled eggs into four plates.

"I'll attest to that," Richard said.

"Is Dad joining us?"

"Yes. At last. He's going to eat quickly then go fishing with that man from Spain," June said, she turned and called for her husband to join them. "Bernard! Breakfast is ready!"

As June called out, he emerged from the doorway, hobbling slightly with the aid of a walking stick. His greying hair added a touch of wisdom to his appearance, while the lines on his face spoke of a life filled with stories.

"Dad, it's great to see you," Philip greeted. "I can't believe you still go fishing with that leg of yours."

Bernard chuckled, his eyes crinkling with amusement. "Well, son. The fish don't seem to mind." Carefully, Bernard made his way to the table, his steps measured and deliberate.

June gazed at her husband with a loving smile. "You know your father, always determined to cast his line, no matter what. It's one of the things I love about him."

Bernard took his seat, his presence radiating a quiet strength. His weathered hands, roughened by years of outdoor pursuits, carried the marks of countless fishing trips and adventures.

"Congratulations my boy. Your mother told me about your publishing deal. I'm proud of you."

"Thanks, Dad."

"Just a word of advice from an old man. Be careful. Publishers have been known to be sharks."

"Not this one, Dad. They've explained everything to me and I'm happy with the contract."

"How much did they advance you?"

"One and a half mil."

"Very nice. I wish you everything of the best, my boy."

While they ate and exchanged small talk about the weather and the state of fishing in the area, Philip was reserved, saying very little, and he nibbled at his food while the others gobbled the breakfast down as if it was their last meal. While June cleared the table, and Bernard went to meet the man from Spain, Richard turned to Philip and said, "What's going on. You're too quiet."

"My publisher called me this morning. It seems the author who was supposed to lead a four-week writer's workshop is ill and can no longer manage it. Silas wants me to step in and help out, but he needs an answer by midday. The workshop starts tomorrow."

"Silas? You mean Silas Turner from Bolt Publishing?"

"Yes, do you know him?"

"I've worked on a number of books for him. They're highly professional."

"That's good to know."

"What's the problem?"

Philip sighed, frustration in his voice. "I have my own business to run. I can't simply drop everything and leave it unattended for a whole month. It's a significant commitment, and I don't know if I can manage it alongside my other responsibilities."

Richard nodded. "I see. It's a tough decision to make. A hell of a challenge."

"Exactly. I love writing, and the opportunity to help others in a writer's workshop is appealing. But at the same time, I need to consider the practicalities and ensure my business continues to thrive. Emma can't do it alone."

Silence settled between them as Philip contemplated the potential outcomes of his decision.

"I would suggest you talk to Emma first before making a decision," Richard said, picking up Philip's cell phone from the table and handing it to him. Philip punched in her number and waited a moment.

"Hi, Em."

"What's wrong?" she said, recognizing the concern in his voice.

"Can I meet you at Llandudno in an hour?"

# Chapter 10

Emma found Philip at his desk, typing away on his computer. She stood at the door and stared at him for a while before he looked up and noticed her.

"What? No good morning?" she said, approaching him. "How was Cape Point?"

"I loved it. Something important has come up. Silas wants me to run a writer's workshop for a month."

Emma's eyes grew wide. "A whole month? Are you serious? What about the business?"

Philip's smile faltered as he tried to reassure her. "I know it's a big commitment, but this workshop is a fantastic opportunity for me."

Frustrated, Emma crossed her arms. "I get that it's an opportunity, Philip, but what about our clients? What about the events we have lined up?"

Philip's enthusiasm waned as he considered Emma's concerns. "Bolt believes this workshop could be a game-changer for me."

Emma said, "I can't believe what I'm hearing right now. We've worked so hard to build this business together. Our clients rely on us. How can you just leave everything behind for a month?"

"I thought you'd understand and support me."

"Of course, I want you to succeed, Philip. But this workshop feels like it's overshadowing everything we've built. Can't you negotiate a shorter timeframe or find a compromise?"

Philip hesitated, realising the impact his decision could have on their partnership. "I'll talk to Silas and see if there's any flexibility. But I can't guarantee anything. I'll do my best to find a solution. I'll talk to Silas."

"You know what? Damn this business. Maybe we should close down?"

Philip's face filled with anxiety. "I can't believe you just said that."

Emma crossed her arms. "Philip, I've supported you through thick and thin, even when you were writing your book. But now that you have this newfound success, you want to abandon everything we've built together?"

Philip's tone grew defensive. "It's not about abandoning anything, Emma. This writer's workshop is a huge opportunity for me. And it's more money."

Emma's eyes welled up with tears. "This is not just about the money. Wedding Bells is our passion, our livelihood."

"I know."

"And what about our friendship? What about the countless hours we've spent together? Are you willing to throw it all away?"

Philip's gaze dropped to the floor, his words barely a whisper. "No, I don't want to lose our friendship. I need your support, Emma."

"It feels like you're choosing your writing career over everything else. I thought we were in this together, but now it seems like the business is just an afterthought."

"Wedding Bells is not an afterthought. I care about the company deeply. But I also have dreams and aspirations."

"Maybe it's time for us to re-evaluate our priorities, Philip. If your writing career is truly what matters most to you now, maybe it's best for us to part ways."

"Are you listening to yourself?"

Emma's voice trembled. "I'm saying maybe it's best for both of us to move on. I can't keep waiting in the shadows while you pursue your dreams. It's time for me to find my own path."

She turned and walked out of Philip's cottage. He ran after her, calling out her name, trying to get her to stop but she climbed into her car.

"Emma, wait!" Philip grabbed the door handle as she was about to slam it shut. "I'm trying to tell you nothing has changed."

"Do you think I'm stupid? I wasn't born yesterday? We have bookings scheduled for the whole fucking month and you expect me to do it all alone because you need to find yourself as a published author? No, Philip. I think you've made up your mind. You say nothing has changed, then don't phone me next week and say something different. Because if you do, I'll fucking cut your private parts out and feed them to the whales. That's not an idle threat." She turned the ignition and sped away, tyres screeching along the road, leaving him to figure out what just happened.

Of course, Emma was frustrated and angry. In her eyes, Philip had abandoned his commitments to the company, but there seemed to be something deeper. Could it be that she regretted pushing him to have his work published, because now she had accused him of prioritizing his writing over their shared responsibilities. It was obvious that she was deeply hurt by his decision to take on the writer's workshop.

Philip, confused and uncertain about their relationship and the consequences of his choices, punched in Richard's number and spoke to him on his phone.

"Hi there, this is a surprise," Richard said.

"I just spoke with Emma, and she wants out of the business and our friendship."

Richard listened attentively, his brow furrowing with concern. "I'm sorry, Philip. It must be difficult for you. But remember, your writing career is also important. This writer's workshop is an opportunity to put yourself on the literary map."

Philip sighed, his mind grappling with the situation. "I know, Richard, but I'm worried about balancing my business and the workshop. It feels like a lot to handle."

"Talk to Emma. Tell her to hire someone to assist then you can focus on the workshop without neglecting your responsibilities."

Philip's face brightened, considering the possibility. "It might bring us back on the same page."

"Absolutely. I'm sure you can find a way to make it work and your business will continue to thrive."

With Richard's plan in mind, Philip ended the call and sent Emma a message:

*I'm taking on this workshop Em. In the meantime, I want you to run the show and employ someone who knows what he's doing to help you. I love you. Hugs*

Then he sent a message to Silas: *I'll do it.*

A few moments later Philip received a message: *Great! See you within the hour at your place.*

***

In his classroom, Richard was unusually silent, staring at the wall. His mind was in chaos. He had never believed in love at first sight before, but meeting Philip had challenged his belief. He had heard stories from friends about love at first sight. Now, for the first time, he realised he had changed and evolved.

"Mr. Richard?" A voice from one of the students interrupted his thoughts. "Mr. Richard, are you okay? You're just staring at the wall."

Richard leaped into action as if he had just woken up from a long sleep. "Sorry, class. Okay, without further ado, let's do this." He slid the board to reveal the quote he had written earlier. It was from "The Notebook", by Nicholas Sparks. He read the quote out loud. "I am nothing special; just a common man with common thoughts, and I've led a common life. There are no monuments dedicated to me, and my name will soon be forgotten. But in one respect, I have succeeded as gloriously as anyone who's ever lived: I've loved another with all my heart and soul, and for me, that has always been enough."

A young girl with a blonde ponytail put up her hand.

"Susan," Richard said.

"Sir, I can't understand why the author writes 'gloriously'?"

"Okay, let's look at the quote. Firstly, it captures the essence of Noah Calhoun's perspective on love and the depth of his feelings for Allie. It showcases his belief that love is a profound and significant achievement in life, regardless of other worldly accomplishments or recognition. So whatever Noah has done, whether it be building a house, or even going shopping, or loving his parents, or his new blue jeans, nothing compares quite closely to the feeling of love. It's so deep that it transcends everything, hence the reason he uses the word 'gloriously'."

"Thank you, sir."

"Let's read on, shall we? Open your books to page 95 and Caleb, please start."

"One more question, sir." A voice from the back of the class came from a young man who usually didn't say much.

"Yes, Frank."

"Back to the quote on the board. How does Noah know if it's love if he has never been in love before?"

Richard pondered the question, his mind drifting to Philip. "He knows because he can't sleep, or eat or drink or visit family or just do the simple things in life without thinking about Allie. She's captured his heart. It hurts him when she's not around, it eats him from the inside out and he has butterflies whenever he sees her. Everything else has no meaning or consequence."

And that's precisely what Richard felt for Philip.

A small voice from the middle of the room interrupted him. "But, sir, sometimes I have to do things without the person I love. I mean that's normal, isn't it?"

"Sure," Richard said. Reflecting for a moment, he paused. Philip had captured his heart, the longing to be with him, to hold him close, was a constant whisper in his mind. He continued, "We all have to do things without the other person. But it leaves an ache in our chests, an emptiness that speaks volumes about our feelings. It's like a vital part of us is missing whenever our love isn't around."

"But sometimes I feel the same way about friends," the same student said.

"We all love our friends. But the love we're discussing now is the love we feel for someone who has become the centre of our world. Without them, the world seems to stop."

And in that moment of retrospection, Richard could no longer deny his feelings any longer. The magnitude of his emotions demanded action. Philip was more than just a friend. He was someone Richard wanted to share his life with.

He had to do something about it before it was too late.

And then he remembered what Philip had said at dinner: *I can never love a pilot again.*

# Chapter 11

Silas noted the simple and understated furnishings in Philip's living room: A sleek sofa, a functional desk with a computer, and a couple of carefully chosen pictures of family adorned the walls. The cottage exuded a sense of minimalism, allowing the breath-taking view of the ocean and Table Mountain to take centre stage. His eyes landed on a picture capturing a kiss between Philip and another man. "Is this Mike?"

Philip's expression shifted, sadness flickering in his eyes. "That's Mike."

Silas's tone softened. "Good looking guy."

Philip nodded, a touch of nostalgia in his voice. "He was. We shared many beautiful moments together. Shall we get down to business?"

They settled into a comfortable conversation, brainstorming ideas and outlining the course structure. Silas leaned back in his chair, his eyes gleaming with anticipation. "This workshop is more than just teaching writing techniques. It's about igniting a spark within aspiring writers, helping them create stories to captivate readers' hearts. Your unique perspectives and experiences can inspire them to delve deep into their own potential."

"Exactly what I hope to achieve. Each writer has a voice uniquely their own, and it's through embracing their own stories they can connect with readers. I'll encourage them to tap into their emotions and use that vulnerability to create compelling narratives."

Silas nodded, impressed with Philip's vision. "I love your approach."

They continued to delve into the course material, discussing exercises, writing prompts, and fine-tuning the structure to ensure the workshop's success. The clock ticked away, and as the afternoon turned into night they worked tirelessly, pouring their creativity and expertise into shaping the workshop curriculum.

"Jack's going to love this," Silas said with a smug smile on his face.

"Jack?" Philip asked.

"My husband and partner."

"I had no idea you were gay."

Silas leaned back in his chair, crossing his arms confidently. "The moment I met Jack it was love at first sight. Make no mistake about it, he can be dramatic at times, but really his bark is worse than his bite."

"I'd like to meet him sometime."

Silas closed his laptop and stood up to leave. "I'm sure you will. I think we've developed a great opener for the workshop. I'll see you tonight. Try to be a little earlier to discuss the finer points of the lecture, okay?"

"Sure. I'll be there at six."

***

Philip stood at the podium in the vast auditorium of the University of Cape Town. The room buzzed as all twenty-eight delegates settled into their seats. As he scanned the room, he was surprised to spot Richard among the aspiring writers. Philip smiled, grateful for the familiar face. Clearing his throat, he took a moment to gather his thoughts. "Thank you all for being here today," he began, his voice projecting throughout the auditorium. "My name is Philip Mitchell, and for those who want to know, yes, I am related to Margaret Mitchell, she who wrote, 'Gone with the Wind.'"

"I'm new to lecturing. Bolt Publishing just recently accepted my debut novel so I guess you'll all be wondering what the hell a *debut* writer knows about writing. Nothing much. But, like you, I had to start somewhere. I've rewritten and revised countless times, and even terminated projects of sixty thousand words because of quality."

"I think a great way to start this project is to quote several writers who have reached writing's godhead. One particularly useful quote is this one." He opened a green board behind him and read the words out loud. "'To write well, you must be willing to write badly first. Embrace the messiness of the first draft, knowing that revision is where the magic happens.' What does it mean? Anyone?"

Richard put up a hand and said, "It means it's okay to make mistakes. The first draft may not be perfect or polished but perfection comes when the writer revises and edits."

"You're spot on. Thank you. The phrase, 'write badly first', means that when starting a new piece of writing, it's okay if the initial attempt is not up to your desired standards. It acknowledges writing is a process and the first draft is often just the beginning. It's okay to embrace the messiness of the first draft, understanding that it's a natural part of the creative journey. It's about giving yourself permission to make mistakes, experiment, and explore different ideas without the pressure of perfection."

"The quote also suggests the real magic of writing happens during the revision process. Revision allows for fine-tuning, restructuring, and polishing the initial draft, ultimately leading to a more refined and compelling final piece of writing."

"But, it's also about perseverance, acceptance of imperfection, and the power of revision in the writing process." He posed a thought-provoking question, "What is in your head right now?" Philip asked, his voice filled with gentle curiosity. "What is your ego telling you about yourself? How many of us stop writing because we think we're incapable, especially while writing the first draft?"

He allowed the question to simmer, inviting the participants to reflect, to explore the narratives they had constructed around themselves. The room grew still as each writer grappled with their own introspection, contemplating the significance of their inner dialogue.

Philip continued, "Our ego can shape our perception of ourselves as writers. It can bring self-doubt or fuel our confidence. But remember, it's essential to recognize and challenge the limiting beliefs that may block your growth. We all have potential. We all have unique stories and the first draft is more often than not, *not* the story you want to share. It's going to change, not once, but several times and these changes may question your ability. So why do you write? And be honest folks."

Some answers came from the floor: To express my creativity and imagination; writing allows me to share my stories with others; passing on knowledge and experiences. Philip agreed with all of them, but the one he believed hit the nail on the head, had not been mentioned.

"Amazing, isn't it. Every one of us has a different reason to write. Personally, I write for money. Now, isn't that a sure-fire motivation?" he laughed.

***

At the end of the session he thanked all the delegates for attending. Silas approached him with a bear-hug and, stepping back, said, "You were incredible. I told you this will be a breeze."

"I was as nervous as hell."

"Nervous is good."

A shuffling came from a seat in the auditorium and when Philip looked up, he saw Richard heading towards them.

"Excuse me a moment, Silas."

Silas watched as he headed towards Richard.

"Richard, I'm so glad you're here." Philip said.

"I signed up this afternoon."

"I hope you aren't disappointed with me so far," Philip hugged him.

"I'm loving it. You're amazing."

"Richard?" Silas approached them.

"Silas! Haven't seen you in a few months. How are you?"

Silas extended a hand. "I'm doing well. I didn't expect to see you here." Turning to Philip, he continued, "Richard edited Grey Mattison's book, 'The Invincible Charm of a Romantic Magician.' He did a beautiful job. Richard, why don't you pop by my office tomorrow morning because I'd love you to work on Philip's manuscript? Turn it into a true thing of beauty."

Richard gazed at Philip who silently mouthed the word, "No."

"I'd love to," Richard said, ignoring Philip's unspoken demand.

"Well then, see you tomorrow around three?"

"Perfect."

Taking Philip by the elbow, Silas escorted him to the exit saying, "I think we should get a good night's sleep. Tomorrow is going to be a hell of a day with your second lecture."

# Chapter 12

In his cottage, Philip contemplated the recent events. Richard's unexpected presence at the workshop had caught him off guard. Upon deeper reflection, he recognized that Richard did share a common interest with him; after all, Richard was an English teacher, and a writer. However, he questioned what he could possibly offer Richard that he didn't already know. Philip didn't particularly mind Richard's presence, but what truly bothered him was that both Richard and Silas were eager to edit his manuscript.

That was something he simply couldn't allow.

Lost in his thoughts he was oblivious to the sound of the doorbell. After a brief moment, he finally snapped out of his reverie and made his way to the door. Opening it, he found Richard standing there, a smile on his face.

"I thought it would be nice to catch up over dinner," Richard said, smiling.

"I've already ordered Uber Eats. They're on their way. Come on in." It wasn't only exhaustion: it was his tone of voice, almost contemptuous, like thin ice cracking.

"Is there something wrong?" Richard said, cocking his head to the side.

With a deep breath, Philip let his feelings surface. "How could you, Richard?" he exclaimed.

"What do you mean?"

"When Silas hired you to edit my novel, I told you to say no, but you said yes."

Richard tried to explain, "Publishing houses use editors, and I believe it will enhance your work."

"I've worked tirelessly on my book. I've self-edited it to perfection. I told Silas it doesn't need editing. Yet, you both ignored me."

"In any creative process, there's always room for improvement," Richard said.

Philip's face contorted with frustration. "You're not listening! This is *my* work, *my* creation. I don't want it touched by anyone else. Can't you understand?"

Richard struggled to find the right words. "I made a mistake, sorry."

"Sorry won't undo what's already been done," Philip retorted.

Richard crossed his arms. "You know, I listened to you at the workshop earlier and you said something so true. Many writers write for money, and like you said, you're one of them…"

"What's your point?"

"My point is if you don't have a polished manuscript, you're not going to make any money. It will affect your future work and your relationships with other publishers. Besides, look around you. You have this amazing cottage on one of the most beautiful beaches in the world, you have everything yet, by your own admission you still do things for money."

"Now you're treading on dangerous ground, Richard. Don't go there. My financial status has nothing to do with you."

"I see, is it because you never worked for it? Because Mike left you a fortune?"

"That has nothing to do with you."

"That's because everything's about you, Philip. Only you."

Philip's blood boiled. He pointed to the door. "Right now, I think it's best if you leave. There's nothing more to discuss."

At the door, Richard said, "I'll call Silas and tell him I've had second thoughts."

"Whatever," Philip said, his voice weary and defeated.

He watched as Richard climbed into his SUV and drove off. Writing this book had been an intensely personal endeavour, a journey of self-discovery and creative expression. To Philip, the novel was more than just a collection of words; it was an extension of himself, a piece of his heart laid bare for the world to see. Control and ownership were at the core of his reluctance to involve an editor. He wanted to retain complete authority over every aspect of the book, from the smallest nuances of prose to the overarching themes weaving through its chapters. The thought of someone else tinkering with his words filled him with unease, as if he would be surrendering a piece of his identity in the process.

What if the essence of his voice was lost amidst the changes? What if the delicate balance he had achieved was disrupted, leaving behind something unrecognisable to him?

He felt a deep conviction that nobody could ever understand his vision as intimately as he did. Yet, beneath all these reasons lay the ghosts of past negative experiences. He had once entrusted his work to an editor who had not understood his artistic vision, stifling his voice and imposing changes leaving him disillusioned. The encounter had left a lasting impact on him, one that now fed his reluctance towards external editing. He had chosen a solitary path, relying on his own judgement and instincts to refine his manuscripts.

Silas did not understand, neither did Richard.

# Chapter 13

Silas glanced up from his desk. "Thanks for coming, Richard. Please, take a seat."

Richard cleared his throat, trying to steady his voice. "I met with Philip last night after the workshop and he's adamant. He doesn't want his book edited."

Silas raised an eyebrow. "I know you can convince him to see things differently."

Richard shifted uncomfortably in his seat, choosing his words carefully. "I approached him to discuss his manuscript and he made it abundantly clear he won't allow it."

"How well do you two know each other?"

"His mother introduced us last week at a wedding."

Silas leaned back in his chair, a thoughtful expression crossing his face. "Not long. So, Philip has a strong aversion towards your involvement in his work?"

"Yes. He has closed himself off."

"You need to get him to understand editing is not an option."

Richard studied Silas for a moment, assessing his words. "Silas, that's *your* responsibility, not mine."

"I need your help here, Richard. I'll have a word with him too. In the meantime, I'll get Mary to send you the manuscript via email. You'll have it by the time you get home. Are you attending lectures tonight?"

"I paid for it. I'll be there," Richard said, walking to the door.

# Chapter 14

Richard arrived early and took his usual seat at the back. Attendees settled into their seats as Philip entered and opened the session. "Good evening, everyone. Thank you for being here once again. That means I didn't bore you last night. Tonight, I want to discuss common errors we novice writers often make in our manuscripts." He delved into a lively discussion about overusing adverbs and how they weaken prose, sharing examples of stronger alternatives. He showed them how using strong adverbs enhanced their work. How passive voice and indirect verbs, blocks of narrative, modifiers and qualifiers, all destroyed the pacing in their work.

He asked for their input, and several participants raised their hands. However, when Richard raised his hand to share his thoughts, Philip's eyes shifted, dismissing him without a word. Philip continued the discussion, delving into the pitfalls of all the points he had mentioned.

During the break Richard approached him in the corridor. "Tonight's workshop is enlightening. I wanted to discuss some of the points you raised, but it felt like I couldn't get a word in during the session."

"Richard, you're a teacher. What do you think you can learn from me, a spoiled, rich, spoon-fed pompous brat? I'm wondering why you bothered to show up for this course in the first place, but never mind, you're here."

"I said those words in anger, and I apologise."

Philip crossed his arms, his expression still clouded with resentment. "Apologise? You think saying sorry will make everything okay?"

Richard took a deep breath, trying to maintain his composure. "I truly regret what I said. I want to make amends and have a civilized conversation with you about the topics discussed in the workshop."

Philip scoffed, his voice dripping with sarcasm. "Oh, now you want to learn from me? After insulting me? It's a little too late don't you think?"

Richard took a step closer to Philip. "I made a mistake, and I let my frustration get the best of me. I was wrong."

Philip turned and walked away. "I have to get back to influence all these people with my pompous, immature ways."

***

Richard's heart sank. He stood there momentarily, unsure of what to do or say and sought alone time in the quiet of a nearby restroom. Overwhelmed by the intense surge of frustration, he couldn't contain his emotions any longer. In a burst of raw emotion, he unleashed his pent-up feelings and hit the wall of the cubicle. The impact reverberated through the confined space. It was a release, a physical manifestation of the emotions that had built up within him.

As the echoes of his actions faded away, he took a deep breath, trying to regain his composure. The intensity of his emotions had taken its toll, leaving him drained, but also somewhat liberated.

***

As the session concluded, the attendees dispersed into small groups to discuss the workshop's key takeaways. Philip, surrounded by a circle of admirers, engaged them in animated conversation. When Philip looked up, he was surprised to see Richard had not left. He approached Philip as the delegates dispersed.

"Can we talk?" Richard said with a smile.

"If you have any questions about tonight's workshop, I'll be glad to discuss them."

"I really would like to talk about last night."

"I'm here to discuss writing, Richard."

Richard took a deep breath. "There's something you don't know about me. I hate conflict and I don't respond well to it. Please stop beating about the bush and tell me what the problem is."

Frustrated, Philip said, "You know how I feel about my work. I won't allow it to be edited and I'm not about to change my mind. When I met you last week, I had no idea it would come to this and it's going to take some time to restore our relationship, not that we had one in the first place."

Richard chose his words carefully. "I respect your desire for control over your writing. But still, I believe there's room for us to find common ground and rebuild our connection."

Philip's eyes narrowed; his expression guarded. He crossed his arms, his expression still clouded with resentment.

Richard said, "I'll be getting your manuscript tonight via email and I thought it would be wise for us to set a timetable to discuss your work."

"You know where I'm staying, you have my number, let me know when you're ready. If I'm busy I'll tell you," Philip said, heading up the steps to exit the auditorium.

"What about us?" Richard said out loud.

As Philip reached the top of the steps, he turned back momentarily, his gaze meeting Richard's. "There is no us."

He disappeared through the exit doors.

***

Left standing alone in the now-empty auditorium, Richard took a deep breath and gathered his thoughts. He refused to let this setback deter him.

He made his way back to his apartment and sat at his desk, fingers poised over the keyboard, ready to receive the manuscript. As he clicked the "open" button, he knew the journey towards restoring their relationship would be fraught with challenges. But he was determined to face them head-on, to prove himself and show Philip the depth of his commitment. For now, all he could do was wait and hope Philip would come around, that they could be friends. Richard was prepared to give it his all, to engage in the necessary conversations, and to build on their relationship.

Despite the uncertainties ahead, Richard knew that sometimes, the greatest growth comes from the most challenging of journeys. And he was ready to embark on this journey, no matter the outcome, in pursuit of his passion and the opportunity to rebuild what had been lost.

The manuscript came through and Richard opened it to page one and began reading. As he delved into the words, he found himself captivated. The opening chapters revealed a mastery of storytelling with a narrative that effortlessly drew him in. The characters came alive on the pages, their emotions palpable and their journeys intriguing. Page after page, the power and depth of Philip's writing swept him away. It was evident Philip had poured his heart and soul into crafting this story. But Silas was right, there were inconsistencies. The work needed polishing.

He punched in Philip's number and waited for a response. After a few rings, Philip's weary voice crackled through the phone. "What is it, Richard?" Philip's tone betrayed his fatigue, and Richard heard a yawn.

"I've just finished reading the first half of the book. Philip, it's absolutely incredible," Richard exclaimed, unable to contain his enthusiasm. But before he could delve into the details, Philip cut him off. "Richard, it's past midnight. Let's discuss this tomorrow."

Realising his oversight, Richard's heart sank. "I'm so sorry, Philip. I didn't realise how late it was. Were you sleeping?"

"Tomorrow, Richard," Philip curtly replied, and the line went silent, leaving Richard to ponder yet another blunder.

# Chapter 15

Philip's phone rang. "Fuck! Who the hell could it be now?" he mumbled. "Mitchell," he answered.

It was Silas Turner. "Philip. I'm actually two minutes away from your house. I'm stopping by for a few minutes."

"Yes, sure. See you in a few," Philip said. *Stopping by? Hi, Philip. It's Silas. Are you busy right now? Do you mind if I stop by?* That would have been the correct way to announce his visit.

Within a few minutes, Silas stood in Richard's lounge dressed casually in jeans and t-shirt.

"Have you spoken to Richard?"

"With reservations, yes."

"And?"

"And what?"

"Are you going to work with him?"

"I still don't see the need for an editor because I've done all the editing there is to do and you've read the work. You said it's perfect." Philip's eyes hardened.

"Editing is part of the publishing process. For instance, your hero, Mike, is too nice."

Philip leaned back, contemplating Silas's words. "But what *you* don't understand is this book is based on a true story, *mine*. And the main character is just that; *too nice*."

"Readers want flawed heroes, not angels. You don't understand the publishing process, do you?"

"But Mike *is* flawed. I am too. Mike is successful and not skilled in rejecting people. He always has only good things to say about everybody."

"That may be, but readers don't want angels all the time. Where is Mike the bad boy?"

"There is no 'Mike the bad boy.'"

"You clearly don't understand the publishing process, do you?"

"I beg your pardon?"

"If you understood the process, you'd know every manuscript that crosses my desk must and will be edited by a professional, qualified editor. It's in the contract. Sit down, Philip," Silas said, pointing to the sofa beside him.

"I'm happy standing."

"You'll want to sit when I tell you this," Silas said, patting the cushion.

Philip's heart almost stopped beating. He clenched his fists and sat down.

"Good man," he paused, "did you actually read the contract?"

Philip hesitated, "No, I took your word for everything you said."

"You *were* given a copy."

"I didn't read it."

"Here's the thing. We've paid you a handsome amount of money for this work. Bolt owns the publication rights. Forever. When I say forever, I mean *your* lifetime plus a certain number of years after your death. It's not what *you* want, it's what Bolt requires."

"Next thing you're going to tell me is what to eat and how to hold my fork."

"Close. You might not know this, but Bolt owns you. Everything you do from the moment you signed the contract, is monitored by us. You move, you find a boyfriend, you buy a house, you buy a dog, you die, you shit or piss, everything comes through us. We represent not only your novel but we also represent you."

Philip looked away from Silas. "I don't believe what I'm hearing."

"It's a fact! You're a product. *Our product.* And we market you and your novel to make a profit."

Philip hadn't expected this level of intensity from Silas. Nor did he expect to be told he was just a product. His voice trembled. "Silas, this isn't just about me. It's also about *your* responsibility, as my publisher, to inform and educate me about the terms and implications of the contract."

Silas's face contorted. "I explained that part of the overheads is employing an editor to work on your story. The contract is what it is. Bolt has invested in your manuscript and *you*, and they expect to have full control over it."

"This situation could have been avoided if we had open and clear communication from the beginning so I can make informed decisions about my work," Philip said. "I think you should go now, Silas. I have a workshop to plan." He went to the door and opened it. Philip's gaze remained steady, silently signalling the end of their discussion.

Reluctantly, Silas stood up. "I understand you are angry. The point is you have no option in this. You *will* work with Richard and you'd best hurry with those edits, failing which we can always use the courts to sort this out, and let me tell you, Philip, you won't win."

With those parting words, Silas walked towards the door, casting one last glance at Philip. "Let's not go there."

# Chapter 16

At the workshop, Philip began with: "As a writer who has experienced the highs and lows of crafting a story, I don't profess to understand the importance of each element in creating a captivating plot. I'm also learning, but here's what I do know..." He was well on his way into explaining all about conflict and rising action when the door opened and Richard entered. He took a seat in the back row. Smiling, Philip continued, "Plotting requires us to harness the power of structure, inject action into every twist and turn, and keep it going through pace and goals and motivation. But we need to get the recipe right. The ingredients are always the same; rising action, climax, resolution, subplots, plot twists, and the profound elements of theme and symbolism. By all means, use these ingredients and abuse them in the first draft. When you revise and edit you will create a thrilling plot and it will be an adventure from start to finish."

A woman in the third row raised her hand. "What are *you* working on next?"

The question caught Philip off guard. "I'm toying with a couple of ideas. Maybe a romance between editor and author. But that's just an idea. Let's talk about ideas for a moment. What is an idea? And be careful here. Remember, an idea is not a plot. Because plot is all about...?"

A voice murmured somewhere. "Conflict." It was Richard.

"Exactly. Without conflict you don't have a plot. And plot is all about action and reaction between the characters, not only in the main story but also in the subplots. And it needs to bring about life changing consequences. And so, a central conflict is paramount in every story. You need to infuse your work with cause and effect. At the end of the day a plot has an antagonist, a protagonist, a conflict and a goal."

A young man asked, "Is it essential to move from idea to plot by writing it all out?"

"Yes. You can write it out in two or three pages or even use a writing program online. Get the outline written and start writing and if you can sum up your book in one sentence then you have a strong enough dramatic concept. Okay, let's all chip in here. What are the recognised plotlines? Revenge is one. Any others?"

Richard started. "Catastrophe."

Other delegates mentioned at random, adventure, love, the chase, grief and loss, rebellion, betrayal, the quest, self-sacrifice, persecution, survival, deliverance, rivalry, discovery and ambition.

"There you have it," Philip said. "And there are many more. Each one of them has a formula, and yes, there are writers who don't go according to formula even though publishers like winning formulas. After the break we're going to talk about how to move the plot forward so enjoy your tea or coffee and I'll see you back here in half an hour."

Richard came forward and walked with Philip to the coffee station.

"Silas visited me today," Philip said, helping himself to a cup of coffee. He offered Richard a cup.

"He said he was going to talk to you," Richard said.

"He did. Left no stone unturned."

"What did he say?"

"Tons of stuff. He reminded me I have a signed contract and they basically own me. He also said if I refuse to work with you, he'll get the courts involved."

"He said that?"

"And a lot more."

"He doesn't mean it, surely."

"I think he does."

"It's a beautifully written piece of work, Philip."

"But?"

"But some passages could be polished to read even better."

"I suppose Silas told you what he wants."

"He didn't tell me anything. All I'm interested in is changing some grammar and maybe look at flow."

"The workshop takes all of my time so that it seems like I'm not a fool when it comes to writing. I don't have time to edit. I edited it all while writing."

"Firstly, you're not a fool, Philip. Second, your writing is almost perfect."

"Jesus! Everyone tells me the same thing and then they say it needs editing. Is there something wrong with my logic?"

"Where is the Philip I met last week? Where are you hiding him?"

Philip ignored him. "I'm not entirely convinced any amount of editing will make the work better."

"But I am," Richard said.

Philip's gaze remained fixed on the table. "I've put so much of myself into this manuscript, Richard, and I'm afraid if we edit it further, it might lose its essence."

Richard leaned forward. "I promise you, I won't let that happen. I know you still hold a deep love for Mike, and you'll never forget him or the love you shared. But holding onto his memory is eating you from the inside out."

Philip gazed up at him, pain etched on his face. "What do you know about true love? All your knowledge comes from two bad relationships and books written by Jane Austen and maybe Mills and Boon. Bridgeton probably turns you on. It's easy to romanticise love when you haven't experienced the heart-wrenching loss that changes your life forever."

Richard took a deep breath. "You're right. Jane Austin had a real connection with love and its many nuances. I don't read Mills and Boon by the way, and yes, I like Bridgeton. I may not know true love in the same way you do, but I've experienced my fair share of relationships on a different level. As humans, we tend to edit out the bad parts and hold onto the good. We focus on the positive aspects, just like in writing, where we edit out the negative and keep the essence of what resonates."

Philip absorbed Richard's words—*edit out the negative and keep the essence.* It was a perspective he hadn't considered before, a fresh angle with which to approach his writing and his emotions. "I didn't think about it quite like that," he said. "I had two editors helping me before on other works. I paid them and expected magic. Instead, I got the exact opposite. Both butchered my writing to the point where even my voice had disappeared. Their input was mundane and unremarkable. Do you see now?"

"I'm genuinely invested in your work and want to help you succeed," Richard said. "I know what I've done goes against your standards of loyalty and trust, and if you're not comfortable with our working relationship, I'll bow out. I'll tell Silas to find someone else and we'll call it a day." Richard punched in Silas's number while Philip pondered his words. Philip placed a hand over Richard's phone and said, "Wait. Maybe we can find a way."

Richard hesitated, his finger hovering above the phone's screen. Philip took a deep breath before speaking. "Maybe I'm wrong."

Richard slowly withdrew his hand from the phone.

"So, what do you think we should do?" Philip asked.

Richard thought for a moment and replied, "Let's take a different approach. Instead of changing everything at once, let's work on smaller edits first to preserve your voice and style."

Richard nodded, liking the idea. "Sounds like a plan."

"Tonight then, after the workshop?"

Philip nodded. "Yes, tonight after the workshop. I'll follow you to your place."

# Chapter 17

In Richard's apartment off Sea Point, Philip swiftly opened his laptop and called up his manuscript. The screen illuminated his face. He glanced at Richard, his gaze sharp and unwavering. "Show me your magic," he said.

Richard shifted in his seat. Gazing into Philip's eyes, he said, "Philip, I... I need to say something first," he began, "I want us to be friends and there are things you need to know. Important things."

Philip, his impatience palpable, displayed little interest in Richard's words. He stared at the manuscript on his screen, ready to delve into the editing process. "I don't have time for this, Richard," he retorted, his words clipped and dismissive. "Do you want to help me edit this or not?"

"Will you listen to me, please?" he pleaded.

"What is there to listen to?"

"How do you feel about me?" he stared directly into Philip's eyes.

"I thought we could get our shit together because I really liked you. Suddenly everyone is against me. Emma wants me out of the company I started and Silas wants to fix a manuscript that's not broken."

"I... I don't know how to say this, so, let me just say it and consequences be damned. Lately you've been a shit towards me. But I can't deny my feelings for you."

For a moment, the room fell into a profound silence. Philip said, "You have feelings for me?

"I've liked you since the moment we met."

"Then why did you agree to edit my work, knowing I didn't approve?"

"I'm sorry, okay," Richard whispered, his voice overflowing with remorse. "I didn't fully consider the implications of my decision. I got caught up in the excitement of the project and the desire to be a part of your life. I made a mistake, and I take full responsibility for it. But please believe me when I say my intentions were never to harm or disrespect you. Back to my original question. How do you feel about me...?"

Richard's mind was consumed by Philip. Every fibre of his being longed for Philip's touch, and the mere presence of the man sent his heart into a wild frenzy of emotions, and it was up to him to seize this chance at love. He would have to summon every ounce of courage and determination to make it a reality.

Before Philip could answer, the doorbell rang. "Expecting someone?" Philip asked with a mischievous grin.

"No one at this time of night," Richard said, ambling to the door.

"Jesse?" he exclaimed on seeing his best friend from years ago. The man's eyes were red and puffy, and traces of tears smudged the makeup on his face.

"I have nowhere to go," Jesse said, his voice strained with emotion. "Andrew kicked me out."

The cuffs of his sequined blouse were stained with the residue of tears. Without a moment's hesitation, Richard invited him inside; he couldn't turn his friend away in his time of need. "Come in," Richard said, placing a comforting hand on his friend's shoulder. "What happened?"

Jesse entered, looking worn and vulnerable. "We had a fight..." He stopped talking the moment he saw Philip. "Oh! I'm sorry, I had no idea you had company."

Richard smiled, "Jesse this is Philip, we're busy editing his novel."

"I can't even begin to think about the other stuff you guys are doing. Glad to meet you, honey," Jesse said, blowing Philip a kiss. "Honestly, I messed up, Richard. I really messed up this time."

Philip stood up. "I best be going, Richard. We can continue tomorrow night."

"It's okay, really. Perhaps four ears are better than one. You're handsome," Jesse sang.

"Thanks. Are you sure?"

"Of course I'm sure. Unless my eyes deceive me, you're a ball-buster, doll. Heartbreaker."

"I meant stay," Philip said.

"Of course. Maybe you can put this drag queen's ills of the fucking world into your next piece."

Richard guided Jesse to the sofa and settled down beside him, positioning himself as a pillar of support.

Before diving into the depths of Jesse's story, Richard's instincts kicked in, prompting him to take action. "First, let me take care of you," Richard offered.

In the kitchen he made three cups of steaming coffee. "Here," Richard said, returning to his friend with a mug in his hands. He handed a cup to Philip.

Sipping his coffee, Jesse began, "I have this impulse, you know," he admitted. "When I feel like doing something, I just go for it." Richard nodded, a silent acknowledgement of Jesse's impulsive nature. "I'm an impulsive bitch..."

"Wait! Hold that thought," Richard said. "I'll be back in a moment." He hurried out of the room and returned with two paper towels, a warm face cloth and a bottle of cold cream. He placed a dollop of cold cream, about the size of a fifty-cent piece, and rubbed it between his palms.

Jesse continued, the words flowing like a rushing river. "I just wanted to go out, have a drink. It wasn't about being an alcoholic or anything. Work has been tough, everyone wants a drag queen lately and I needed a release...."

Gently, Richard applied the cream all over Jesse's face with a paper towel, carefully avoiding his eyes. He massaged the cold cream into Jesse's skin using circular motions to break down the makeup. "Remember when I used to do this for you after a show?" Richard asked, taking his time in sensitive areas.

"You're the best friend I've ever had. I can't forget those days. I told him I wanted to go out, but he wouldn't let me. So, I waited until he fell asleep. Quiet as a mouse, I pushed the car to the gate, avoiding turning the ignition to prevent any noise that would wake him up. Just as I was about to start the engine, he appeared at the garage door."

Richard chuckled at the audacity of Jesse's story. "Damn! You pushed the car to avoid waking him up?" he exclaimed, laughing out loud as he took the face cloth and wiped away the cream and the dissolved makeup. He continued wiping until every trace of makeup had disappeared. "Classic. So... you." He took the other paper towel and wiped away the remaining residue.

"The poor man exploded. Even his eyebrows tried to flee in opposite directions."

Richard continued laughing out loud. "I can see it happening. Man-oh-man you got yourself into a mess."

"So now, I have nowhere to go. I could book into a lodge...," Jesse looked away, straight into Philip's eyes. "Oh my God! Those eyes are to die for."

"You can stay here as long as you need," Richard said. "We'll figure things out together, just like old times."

Jesse gazed at Richard with gratitude in his eyes. "Thank you. I don't know what I'd do without you. You've always been there for me, even when I didn't deserve it."

The words struck a chord in Richard's heart, reminding him of the genuine connections he held dear. Despite his feelings for Philip, he knew the importance of friendship and loyalty. He also realised that helping Jesse through this difficult time was the right thing to do.

"We all make mistakes," Richard said with a warm, comforting smile. "I'm here for you. Do you want me to talk to Andrew? Maybe I can help clear the air."

Jesse waved his hands. "It's okay. He'll miss me, and then he'll realise how sorry he is. Everything will be alright. Maybe he just needs a few days to cool off."

"Here, let me take those high heels off. And the wig. Where on earth did you get this wig, it's so black and puffy? You can shower and sleep in my bed. I'll take the sofa."

As fate would have it, just then, Richard's phone rang. "Talk about the devil," Richard remarked, with irony in his voice, as he handed the phone to Jesse. "It's Andrew."

Jesse recoiled, and, with a wave of hands said, "I don't want to speak to him. Ever!"

Richard understood his friend's hesitation, but also knew the importance of facing the situation head-on. "I have to answer it. What do you want me to tell him?" Richard asked, preparing to navigate this delicate conversation.

"Tell him you haven't seen me. You have no idea where I am. Tell him I wish I were dead rather than talk to him." Jesse said, his voice firm.

Richard took a deep breath, mentally preparing himself for the upcoming exchange, then answered the call with a steady composure. "Hi, Andrew. This is unexpected. How are you?" he greeted, adopting a neutral tone to avoid escalating any tensions.

"Terrible," Andrew's voice echoed from the other end of the line. "Jesse and I had an argument. Is he with you?"

"Actually, yes, he is. He's taking a shower right now. I'll let him know you called."

"Thank God! I thought he might have been picked up by some perv or worse."

"He just got here, so I'll tell him to call you back."

Richard ended the call, his thoughts still partially tethered to the conversation. He turned back to Jesse; his compassionate gaze unwavering despite his friend's evident anger. "He's worried about you. Are you sure you don't want to talk to him?" Richard gently probed.

Jesse's frustration intensified. "He humiliated me, like a hurricane tearing through my caftan. Called me a whore. An alcoholic. Told me people hate me. Do you know what he did two weeks ago? He removed all the mirrors in the house. Every one of them. I know I have a problem with mirrors but he rubs it in every day. I can't help it if I feel the need to change my outfit every time I see myself. Treats me as if I'm some kind of sicko. Kicked me out of a house I pay for," he muttered bitterly. "He can drop dead for all I care. He treats animals better than me."

Richard could see the pain etched across Jesse's face, the hurt running deep. "A psychiatrist with a mirror problem, you should have had the problem diagnosed a long time ago."

"I know. I know. But I don't even know what I look like anymore."

"Fix the problem. Get help."

"Easier said than done."

"Surely shrinks have shrinks."

"Yes, but I'm not going down that path. Enough about me and my mirror kink," Jesse deflected, attempting to shift the focus away from his own turmoil. "What about you? Anyone special in your life?" he asked, removing his green stocking,

"I hope there is someone who feels the same way about me, I guess only time will tell." His gaze slanted towards Philip.

"It's been what, five years now?" Jesse asked.

"Four."

"Come, tell me while I shower," Jesse said, grabbing his hand and leading him to the bathroom. "Yech, I stink so badly with cheap perfume. I'll need to use your nightgown. Tell Philip to come and wash my back."

"I'm not sure he'll be up to that," Richard said.

Jesse undressed and stepped into the shower.

"Where's your bar soap, baby?"

"I use a gel. It's good for my skin."

Jesse extended a hand beyond the shower curtain and took the bottle of gel from Richard. "Tell me what's going on," Jesse said in a soft voice.

Richard contemplated whether he should share the complexity of his feelings for Philip. But he knew Jesse well and trusted him with his emotions "I'm head over heels in love with Philip and I've known him less than two weeks."

"Have you told him?"

"I've told him I have feelings for him, but he hates me."

"Hates you? What happened?"

"It's a long story," Richard sighed, "He's a writer and wedding planner. Bolt Publishers accepted his novel and he doesn't want his work edited at all. He says it's good enough as it is. And it is almost perfect. I've done some work for the publishers so they know how pedantic I am with manuscripts. They asked me to edit his work and although Philip begged me not to, I said yes. Something changed between us, and now, it feels like there's this distance, this barrier he's built between us."

Jesse listened attentively, his empathy evident in his eyes.

"He's just going through a lot of deep, inner issues. But it's all business with Philip. He'll allow me to edit the work, but that's all. Nothing more. He's closed the door on me."

Jesse stated firmly, "If he can't appreciate the amazing person you are, then it's his loss."

"But there's something else. His ex-husband, a pilot, died in an aeroplane crash six years ago and he told me he'd never get involved with a pilot again."

"Oh, dear! Have you told him you fly?"

"No."

"You must tell him."

"If I do, I'll lose him forever."

"Sounds like you've already lost him."

"I'm fighting. If only he'd let go of the past."

"Pass me a towel, baby."

Richard gave him the towel and he wrapped it around his waist and stepped out of the shower. "How do I look?"

"Without the dress and the wig and the make-up you look absolutely stunning, but I've told you before."

Jesse waved his hands. "Yes. Yes. Blah, blah, but I enjoy dressing in drag," he said, staring into the bathroom mirror. "God, how I miss my mirrors."

"So, what should I do?"

"Nightgown?"

Richard took his robe from behind the bathroom door. "Any words of wisdom?"

"I'm glad I came tonight," Jesse said. "I would have bolted a long time back. I think he wants you just as much as you want him. He's a little hurt right now because you broke his trust, but he'll get over it because it's just a little thing and if you play your cards right, he'll forgive you. But you have to tell him you're also a pilot. If he catches you, you've had it."

Richard managed a small smile, touched by Jesse's words of encouragement. "It won't be easy."

"I know. But you have to do it soon. Now give me my phone, let me phone my understanding husband. Maybe Philip just needs some time to come around. If he truly values your friendship, he'll realise what he's missing."

While Jesse spoke on the phone, Richard went through to the lounge. Philip had closed his laptop and was ready to leave.

"I'm sorry about this. I had no idea Jesse would disturb us," Richard said.

"That's okay. We can carry on tomorrow. I best be on my way."

"Hug?"

# Chapter 18

The next morning, Philip awoke to the sound of his mobile phone and checked the message.

*It's clear you have no interest in Wedding Bells, so I intend talking with our lawyers to buy you out.*

Philip promptly called Emma back, his voice filled with determination. "Hi, I just got your message. What's all this about buying me out?"

A heavy silence followed. Eventually she spoke. "What did you expect me to do, Philip? Stand by and watch you destroy the company by your absence. Clients are asking for you."

"Come on, Em! You could tell them I'm on holiday, something at least."

"Oh, sure. Your dog died or something?"

"I've been gone barely four days and you spring this on me. I'm not selling to you or anyone else. I'm still very much a part of my company."

Emma's tone remained calm but firm as she responded, "Do you even know that I've had to employ Tom Ridge? You know Tom, he's a fabulous planner."

"I get that, Em. I've been busy as hell. I mean I never knew a writer's workshop could be so intense. I miss you and I'm still committed to Wedding Bells. When I get back, I'll be ready to jump back in and contribute. After Mike passed, we built this company to what it is today, I'm not going to throw it away."

"To me it feels as if you left us high and dry."

Philip replied, "It seems you're not willing to recognize new things as they come up, Em. If I were in your shoes, I would have given you the time off to convene this workshop. Writing is in my blood and *you*, of all people, should understand."

"Philip, I *do* understand your love for writing. I *do* want to work through this together, but you need to understand I can't do this alone."

"So why bring a lawyer into this?"

"Maybe I went too far there, but we need to redefine our working relationship."

"Without lawyers."

Emma paused, considering Philip's words. "So, when are you coming through to discuss this?"

"I'll see you this weekend. Saturday morning. Breakfast at my place. Jesus, since when did we ever have to make an appointment to see each other, Emma?"

"I apologise for not responding to your messages, Philip. I'm angry. It seemed to me you had absconded."

"You forget I created this business. And with more money in it, we can do bigger things."

"Money isn't everything. But I hear you."

"Bring Tom for breakfast too. I'd like to hear what he can do to improve on what we've built."

"He has lots of ideas. Tomorrow we have a meeting with a new client. Dylan Shaw Graphics. They have a fifteenth anniversary coming up."

"Awesome. It's an opportunity to see how Tom works."

# Chapter 19

Dylan Shaw, a distinguished figure in the graphic design business, greeted Emma and Tom with a soft handshake. Emma had expected a hard, strong hand – everything about him looked solid, concrete; she imagined him in a rugby scrum with his bald head, thick neck and huge arms and chest. Everything about him exuded power.

"Emma, Tom, welcome. I'm thrilled to have you here," he said.

Emma shook his hand with a friendly smile. "Thank you, Dylan. We're honoured to meet you."

Tom, the direct opposite of Dylan, extended a lean arm, and with a toss of his long, blonde hair, he replied," It's a pleasure to be here."

Dylan gestured for them to take a seat. "Let's dive right into it. I understand you're the team that will help us celebrate our fifteenth anniversary in style."

Emma nodded, a glimmer of excitement in her eyes. "We're thrilled to be involved. We've been looking forward to working with you."

Dylan leaned forward, his gaze focused and determined. "I want this event to be unforgettable. It's not just the company's birthday, it's also a moment to show our appreciation to our customers, suppliers, and staff. We want to leave a lasting impression."

Tom chimed in, his voice brimming with confidence. "Rest assured, Mr. Shaw, we understand the significance of this occasion. We've been meticulously planning every aspect, from the venue to the decorations and everything in between."

Dylan nodded, visibly pleased. "Good to hear. The event should also capture our innovative spirit and showcase the artistic essence of our brand. The venue needs to be top-notch, and the aesthetics should be visually captivating. Tell me what you have in mind."

Tom said, "Firstly, I recommend the prestigious Belmond Mount Nelson Hotel for breath-taking views. For elegance, stunning floral designs will add pizazz, and those who want can take the bouquet's home after the event. We'll light up the place and offer a gourmet meal with bespoke cocktails. And there you have it. All supplied by the very best companies to partner you on your birthday."

"Talk to me about the cost," Dylan said, flipping the pages in the file.

"Four hundred thousand including our fee," Tom said.

"Okay. The budget I have is way less than what you think we can afford. Come back to me with a reasonable plan and then we'll talk. I have an EXCO meeting on Tuesday and they'll want to know what we're in for." Dylan said, ushering them to the door.

Emma immediately thought the meeting didn't go well. On the way to the car she said, "He doesn't like our plan, Tom. It's too expensive."

"Too expensive? This guy makes ten million rand profit a month. It's a drop in the ocean for him. I guess you're thinking Philip would have done better, right?"

"Maybe."

"But he's not me, Emma. I give the best. The very best. My clients expect nothing less."

"I don't doubt it, Tom, but let's come up with something else by Sunday night."

***

During the early stages of his writing, Philip told the delegates that evening, he would change viewpoints instead of sticking to one of the tried and tested elements and, as a student, always lost marks in exams because of it. It was only much later he realised his mistake and started writing in the simple past tense using one person's vantage point, third person point of view. "Nowadays," he told his audience, "us poor authors have taken to third-person multiple viewpoints, giving the reader the opportunity to know how all the characters feel by showing multiple thoughts and motivations."

Some agreed with him, others had something to say, most preferred first-person point of view, past tense. Others wrote in second person, allowing the reader to become part of the story. Philip added they should experiment with different points of view and use the one that works best for the story. "Be careful," he said, "of using second person for a full novel. It works best in short stories. Anita Shreve was an author who successfully changed points of view in her novel 'The Weight of Water', if you are able to get hold of a copy it's worth studying and analysing her structure."

***

Afterwards, Richard followed him to his cottage at Llandudno. Inside, Richard said, "Silas wants it finished as soon as possible."

Philip gazed at Richard with a mischievous smile, his eyes sparkling with anticipation. "I'm sure we'll have it finished sooner. How about we break a bottle of wine and get to work? White or red? Sweet or dry?"

Richard chuckled, considering his options. "I'm a softy for sweet white."

Philip grinned, delighted with Richard's choice. "Good choice. I'm a fan of sweet whites too."

Philip headed toward the small wine rack in the corner of the room. "I have a feeling this is going to be a productive and enjoyable evening." he said, a playful glint in his eyes as he returned to the desk, a bottle of sweet white wine in hand. He uncorked it with practised ease and poured the golden liquid into two wine glasses.

"I couldn't agree more," Richard replied.

Philip handed him a glass. They crossed arms and Philip said, "Here's to you, here's to me,

The best of friends we'll always be.

But if by chance we disagree,

To hell with you, here's to me!"

They laughed out loud and clinked glasses together then settled back into their seats. Philip said, "I don't think we'll get through the last half tonight, if not we'll continue tomorrow night, are you available?"

"I'm always available."

"Great stuff. And I have a confession."

"Sorry, not a priest," Richard said.

"Just as well. I know I said the book doesn't need an edit, but the last chapter is a mess. Will you take a look at it first?" Philip said, his expression focused and contemplative. "We need to bring this story to a satisfying conclusion. And it's going to be hell for me. This is where Mike dies."

"I'm wondering if readers, especially women, would read a tragedy. Why don't you give the novel a happy ever after?"

Philip's eyes clouded over. "Life isn't all about happy-ever-afters. Besides, what happened is true."

"Let's just take it one step at a time," Richard said. "From what I read I tend to agree with you. At the end of the last chapter Mike had taken prescribed relaxation tablets the night before he was to fly out. I think it would be irresponsible for him to fly if he was on medication. A pilot's moral duty is the safety of the plane and his passengers."

"He *did take* those tablets. He took them and I only knew the following day when I found the empty bottle lying on the bathroom dresser."

"How many did he take, do you know?"

"The forensic report indicated he took four."

"And they make a person feel drowsy?"

"Yes. Also, the next day you feel like shit."

"Okay, so how did it all pan out?"

Philip began, "The following morning I tried to wake him up. Usually, he'd get up immediately. He had this internal clock but it wasn't working that morning, when he did wake up, he was groggy and cranky. I was concerned. This had never happened before. I wasn't sure if he should fly out."

"What if we give Mike a moment of self-realisation?" Richard suggested. "A moment where he knows he shouldn't take to the skies."

Philip's eyes lit up with enthusiasm. "He actually told me just before leaving that he shouldn't be flying so I brought his bag inside. I didn't want him to go. It was as if he knew. What's the word for it... damn!"

Richard said, "A sixth sense? Perception? Intuition?"

"Intuition! He had this deep-rooted sense of intuition. But, instead of listening to his gut, he ran back inside the house and picked up his bag again."

Richard read out loud:

*"What's wrong with you?" Mike exclaimed, grabbing the bag and rushing out.*

*Philip stood at the front door calling him back, but Mike wouldn't listen. He climbed into his car and raced off.*

*An hour later airport authorities contacted Philip and gave him the news. Mike was dead.*

*He flew his plane into Table Mountain.*

Richard buried his head in the palm of his hands. "That is strong stuff. Suicide?"

Philip held his breath for a moment. He couldn't speak. He turned his gaze to the ocean and only after a minute or two, said, "They couldn't prove suicide."

"Fuck," Richard responded. "I'm speechless."

"I was speechless too."

"It's got nothing to do with me but did insurance pay out?"

"They did. Only after a year of an exhaustive investigation."

"You don't cover that aspect in the book."

"It was ugly. They immersed themselves into my personal life. Drug tests. Handwriting analysis. Camera footage. They wanted to know what time Mike ate supper, had breakfast. They demanded his flight log and interviewed as many clients as they could. They examined the Cessna and were just about to reject the claim when they found something wrong with the plane. The back wing – I don't know what you call it – malfunctioned just after take-off."

Richard said, "It's called the horizontal stabilizer, also known as the tailplane. It provides stability and control to the aircraft during nose-up and nose-down pitch movements. This malfunction after take-off would cause control issues not easily rectifiable during flight. Horrible." He stopped abruptly, realising he had said too much.

"I'll need to include that in the book," Philip said.

They continued working and close to midnight Richard showed him the completed piece.

Philip took a deep breath. "Perfect."

But Richard didn't answer. He was far too busy gazing at Philip.

"Richard? Wakey wakey!"

Richard leaped out of his reverie. "What? Did you like it?"

"Yes. It's perfect. Where were you?"

"I can't imagine how difficult the accident must have been for you," Richard said.

"It was devastating. I loved him with all my heart and I never got the chance to tell him how much he meant to me that day."

Richard reached out and placed a hand on Philip's shoulder. "Sometimes life throws us these unimaginable challenges."

Philip checked the time on his computer and caught himself. "It's late. I think we should call it a day. I'm ready for bed."

Richard collected his cell phone and car keys. "I'll see you tomorrow," Richard said, heading for the door. "Thanks for the wine and the coffee, and the company."

"You could stay," Philip said.

Richard stopped at the door. "Stay? Are you sure?"

Philip closed the door. "It's after midnight. There's no way you're going home. Besides, you're on holiday."

"True."

"I'll prepare the guest bedroom."

# Chapter 20

Philip opened the photo album and slowly turned the pages. In one picture, he and Mike were both grinning widely, standing on the beach in front of the cottage. It was the day Mike bought the place. The wind tousled their hair as they held each other close, their eyes filled with excitement. Another photograph captured them on the beach, their toes buried in the warm sand. He revisited glimpses of birthdays, holidays, and ordinary moments like dining at fancy restaurants.

Tears welled up in his eyes as he held a particular picture of Mike, his face alight with joy, captured in mid-laugh. It was a candid moment of unfiltered happiness, frozen in time. Philip traced his fingers along the edges of the photograph, as if trying to bring to life the man he had lost. He tried to find peace in these photographs. They reminded him of the love they shared, the moments that shaped them, and the impact Mike had on his life. But the tears kept on coming.

"Philip?" Richard whispered from the doorway.

Philip didn't hear him. His sobbing filtered out the whisper. Richard came closer and took him in his arms. "It's okay. It's okay. I've got you."

"We had the future in our hands and he took it away from us in the blink of an eye." Philip lamented, his voice choking.

Richard held him tighter, letting him grieve. "I know it's incredibly painful, losing someone you love. It's not fair, and there are no words to make it right. But remember, you still have your memories and the love you shared. Mike will always be a part of you."

"But it hurts so much," Philip sobbed, clutching onto the photograph as if holding onto a piece of his heart.

Richard gently took the photograph from Philip's trembling hands and stared at it with admiration. "These pictures are a testament to the beautiful life you both had together. The love you shared is evident in every smile, every embrace. That love will never fade, even if Mike is no longer physically with you."

Philip nodded, trying to find comfort in Richard's words. "I just don't know how to move forward without him. I've tried, I really have and all I can think of is I should have been on that plane with him."

"It's okay to feel lost and broken," Richard said softly, wiping away a tear from Philip's cheek. "Grief is a process, no matter how long it takes, and there's no right or wrong way to go through it. Just know that I'm here for you, and you don't have to go through this alone."

For the first time since Mike's passing, Philip felt a glimmer of hope. He leaned into Richard's embrace, and stayed there until the tears stopped.

"Please sleep with me," Philip whispered. "I just need you right now to hold onto."

"I'll hold onto you the whole night long. I promise I won't let you go." Richard replied, offering comfort and reassurance.

They lay side by side in Philip's bed. Richard gently wrapped his arms around Philip, providing a sense of security and warmth.

Richard's voice was filled with care and tenderness. "You're not alone, baby. I'm right here with you, and I'll be here as long as you need me. You're loved, and I'm here to care for you, no matter what it takes."

Philip's touch was both tentative and seeking, as if he was reaching out for connection. His fingers traced delicate patterns on Richard's chest, searching for reassurance and comfort in the embrace. Each touch conveyed a profound need for closeness. In the intimate space they shared, Richard's skin radiated a warmth where physical touch transcended words, and spoke volumes about the depth of their emotions and the solace they found in each other's presence.

***

In the morning, a gusty south-easterly prevailed and Richard watched from the patio as several surfers took advantage of the ocean swell and the tall waves breaking along the shoreline.

"Do you surf?" Philip asked, handing Richard a cup of coffee and a plate of toast.

"Never tried," Richard replied with a smile, accepting the coffee and toast. "It looks exhilarating."

Philip nodded, sipping his own coffee. "It is. I used to surf with Mike all the time. It was one of our favourite things to do together. Sometimes, I wish I could go back to those carefree days."

"Are you up for it?" Richard suggested. "I'd love to watch you surf."

Philip looked out at the crashing waves, he appreciated Richard's interest in wanting to be a part of something that was so meaningful to him. "I'm not sure if I'm ready to surf again just yet. It's still a little too raw for me."

"I think *you are* ready. Come on, let's do this."

Philip hesitated for a moment before making up his mind. "You want to learn?" he asked.

"A new challenge. I'm always up for that."

"I see. So you also regard me as a new challenge then?"

Richard's eyes crinkled with a hint of amusement. "A new challenge, huh? You know what they say, Philip, the best way to grow is to take on new challenges." Richard pointed at the ocean. "Look at those guys. Each guy better looking than the next one."

Philip pretended to slap him. "Stop looking at them. Your head's gone south."

"I'm kidding, but they're definitely in shape."

Philip yawned, "Boring. Let's get the surfboards."

They retrieved the surfboards from the storage room and Philip noticed the apprehension in Richard's eyes. "Are you sure you want to do this?"

"I'm sure."

"Alright, before we hit the water, there are a few things you need to know about prepping the surfboard," he began. "First check for damage on its surface for dings, cracks, or any signs of wear," Philip explained, showing Richard how to carefully examine the board. "Do you see any cracks?"

Richard carefully inspected his board. "I don't see any."

"Good. That means you're good to go." He filled a bucket with fresh tap water and got hold of a soft brush. "After every surf session, you'll need to rinse the board with fresh water to remove sand and saltwater. But don't press hard. Use the brush gently to get rid of any stubborn dirt otherwise you'll damage the board's surface."

Richard nodded, absorbing the information as he followed Philip's lead. "Got it, clean the board after each session. Don't press hard with the brush."

Philip continued. "When you're satisfied the board is safe and clean, you have to wax it. The wax provides traction to grip the board better while surfing."

Philip took a spoonful of wax into a clean cloth and rubbed his board using small circles to create a textured layer. Richard did the same.

As Philip applied the wax to his own board, he said, "You want to make sure the wax is evenly spread, giving you a good grip when you're out there on the waves."

"Next, we check the fins," Philip said, pointing to the bottom of the surfboard. "Ensure they're securely attached and the fin setup is suitable for the conditions you'll be surfing in."

Richard examined the fins, making sure they were tight and secure. "I'm good to go on this part."

Philip smiled, impressed by Richard's quick grasp of the process. "Great job. Now, don't forget your leash." He held up a surfboard leash for Richard to see. "This is crucial for safety. It connects your ankle to the board, preventing it from drifting away if you fall off. *And you will fall.*" Philip giggled.

Richard took the leash and attached it to the plug on his surfboard. "Got it, safety first."

The storeroom was filled with the scent of sea breeze and a faint aroma of sunscreen as Philip smiled warmly at Richard, handing him a pair of blue trunks. "Hope you like blue," he said as he opened a drawer filled with various items of clothing and towels.

Richard grinned as he took the trunks from Philip's outstretched hand. "As long as it fits, I'm happy," he replied.

Philip carefully selected a pair of black trunks for himself. He undressed and the cool air from the open window gently brushed against his skin, sending a shiver down his spine. When he looked up, Richard was staring at him.

"What?"

Richard quickly looked away. "Nothing."

"You were looking at me change. Like what you see?"

"Fuck, yes."

"Tease."

Philip's heartbeat quickened. He had also taken a glimpse of Richard's naked body as he changed and was impressed by each curve and muscle. He grabbed a bottle of tanning lotion and opened it. The scent of coconut mixed with the salty sea air.

"I'll rub you down. The sun can be intense," he advised. He squeezed the lotion onto his hand and felt the smooth texture between his fingers. He gently rubbed the suntan lotion onto Richard's warm skin, taking care to spread the lotion evenly, using gentle strokes. The smoothness of Richard's skin created a sense of intimacy beyond words and he felt a rush of excitement flow through his body. There were no boundaries, but he kept his feelings in check, understanding that this act of applying sunscreen was purely for Richard's protection and not an invitation for anything more. His hands spread lotion across, over and between Richard's thighs and calves, his back, chest and neck and by the time he was done he quickly turned away to conceal his erection. He handed the bottle to Richard.

Richard accepted the lotion gratefully and applied it to Philip's skin with careful consideration. The moment Richard's hand connected with his skin, Philip trembled slightly.

"You have goosebumps," Richard laughed.

"Your hands."

"Hmm, I'll remember that. You have a beautiful body."

"Flattery will get you everywhere."

"I hope so."

Philip closed his eyes as Richard slowly rubbed the lotion all over, from his toes right up to his forehead. His heart pounded with excitement. This moment was more than just surfing; it was a connection of souls, a shared experience that would create lasting memories.

With everything in place, Philip led Richard to a quieter spot on the beach, away from other surfers. "Now, before we venture into the water, let's practice the waxing and attachment of the leash a few more times. It's important to get comfortable with these steps before heading out."

For the next ten minutes, Philip patiently guided Richard through the process until he felt confident enough to tackle the water. They carried their boards to the beach, and Philip noticed the look of wonder in Richard's eyes as he admired Philip's physique.

Once they reached the shoreline, Philip took a deep breath, trying to calm his nerves.

"Remember, take it step by step, and don't be afraid to ask for help if you need it," Philip said.

The rhythmic ebb and flow of the tides seemed to synchronize with the beat of their hearts and, with the sun warming their skin and the waves beckoning them forward, they shared a nod of determination. As they waded into the water, the waves crashed around their legs, and Philip felt the rush of adrenaline building within him.

"I'm here for you every step of the way," Philip said, giving Richard a supportive smile. He had surfed countless times with Mike, and he didn't want fear to hold him back now.

The waves crashed around them, and Philip felt the familiar sensation of the ocean's backwash power beneath his feet. "Just follow my lead, okay. We're going to lie on the board and paddle out beyond the first waves."

"I'm right behind you," Richard said.

"And if you don't want to stand, you can belly surf the wave. But try to catch the same wave, okay?"

"Sure thing. I'll probably belly surf for now."

Finally, a suitable wave approached, and Philip felt it adrenaline rushing through him. He paddled hard, positioning himself on the board. The wave lifted him, and for a brief second, he felt a connection to the past, to the joyous times he had spent surfing with Mike.

He rode the wave with grace and determinations while Richard cheered him on from behind, his body prostrate on the board as he rode the same wave, and Philip smiled gloriously.

They spent the morning surfing and laughing, while Richard tried standing, but fell over and over again. Philip lost all trace of Mike's memory. It was like Mike never existed.

As they returned to the beach, Philip felt he had accomplished something. Surfing with Richard had been healing. "Thank you," Philip said, his voice filled with gratitude. "I couldn't have done it without you."

Richard smiled, "You did great out there."

As they walked towards the cottage, ready to face an afternoon of editing, Philip was stronger than ever before. With Richard by his side, he could navigate the highs and lows of life, cherish the memories of the past, and embrace new experiences. He realized healing wasn't about forgetting the past; it was about finding the courage to create new moments of joy.

***

While Philip showered to rid his body of the sea salt, Richard put on the TV and searched for a mix on You Tube, starting with Shayne Ward's 'Stand by Me', and moving on to other feel-good songs. His entire body ached, not from exhaustion, but with a warmth for being close to Philip. The experience of sharing the waves, the sun, and the ocean with him had deepened their bond and he appreciated every moment. He was comfortable. While he may not have fully understood the complexity of Philip's emotions, he felt a genuine connection between them; it made him feel wanted. His love stronger. He wanted to grow old with him. Share in his success. Bring him happiness. Have a family and die in his arms. But, for that to happen, he'd need to tell him he was also a pilot and he'd need to choose the moment carefully.

***

The rest of the week went by quickly. Richard and Philip worked on the novel together, starting from the first page. They took turns reading each word out loud. Sometimes, Richard would stop and show a grammar or spelling mistake or typo.

"Grammar Nazi," Philip laughed.

During their breaks, they would go surfing. Richard quickly improved his skills, despite stumbling every time he tried to stand up on the board. They laughed out loud each time, but Richard was determined to master it. And every day Silas phoned to find out how far they had come.

But when Friday arrived, Richard noticed a shift in Philip's mood. He seemed different.

"Want to go for a walk along the beach?" Richard asked. The waves crashed gently on the shore as they strolled in the soft sand. The salty breeze mixed with the warm sun.

Richard waited for the right moment before gently inquiring, "Is everything okay?"

Philip sighed, his gaze fixed on the horizon. "It's just... I've been thinking about some things. Us."

Richard nodded, giving Philip space to express his thoughts.

"I mean, we've been having a great time, but I wonder what happens after this week. We'll go back to our regular routines, and I don't want things to change between us."

Richard listened, understanding Philip's words. The bond they had developed during these five days was strong, and the thought of it fading away was unsettling.

"I feel the same way," Richard admitted. "This week has been incredible."

They walked in silence for a while, the sound of the waves providing a soothing backdrop.

"I guess what I'm trying to say is," Philip started, vulnerability in his voice, "I hope we can make an effort to stay close, even when life gets busy."

Richard smiled, appreciating Philip's honesty. "I'm on the same page, I don't want this to end."

"Will you stay at least a few more days?" Philip asked, gazing into Richard's eyes.

"I never thought you'd ask. Yes. I'd like that very much."

Philip, in a moment of longing, leaned in closer until their lips met. His heart swelled with a deep sense of longing and desire. As he leaned in closer, his entire body tingled with anticipation. The gentle brush of their lips meeting sent a rush of warmth surging through him. It was a tender and affectionate gesture, filled with unspoken emotions. In that brief encounter, the world seemed to fade away, leaving only the profound connection they shared.

"Do you have any idea what you do to me, Philip Mitchell?"

"Roughly."

Richard returned the kiss, but this time his tongue swirled inside Philip's mouth. Philip's senses were ignited, and he welcomed Richard's advances with a sigh of pleasure. The taste of Richard's lips and the electrifying sensation of their tongues entwined sent a shiver of excitement coursing through him. In that intimate embrace, they explored each other's depths, their connection deepening with every breathless moment, as if they were unlocking a newfound intimacy that had long been yearned for.

They parted and Richard said, "I wanted to kiss you on the balcony at the wedding. Damn! You're fucking amazing, Philip Mitchell."

They continued on their walk hand in hand when Philip said, "Tomorrow I'm going to need some alone time. I usually stop at Mike's grave first thing every Saturday morning. Afterwards I have a meeting with Emma, and tomorrow afternoon a quick visit to Cape Point. June wants to see me about something."

"What time will you be back?"

"In time for dinner. Is that okay with you?"

"I'll spend the day on your manuscript. Really polish it up."

"I trust you, Richard. I know you'll do what's best for the manuscript. I'll try to be back as soon as I can. I promise. I don't want to spend too much time away from you."

As the sun began to set, casting a warm glow across the ocean, both continued their walk. Both knew they had crossed the line and there was no turning back

# Chapter 21

On Saturday morning Philip arrived at the cemetery just as the gates opened, a solemn and contemplative expression on his face. He made his way towards the florist located conveniently by the side of the cemetery.

The bell chimed softly as he entered the small shop, the scent of flowers enveloping him. His eyes scanned the colourful array of blooms, but he knew exactly what he needed. He walked towards a stand filled with white roses, their delicate petals pristine and elegant.

A voice came from behind the counter. "They're on special, sir. Beautiful, aren't they?"

"Yes, they're absolutely magnificent."

Philip pulled a fresh bunch from its tin container and handed it to the Indian man behind the counter.

"You come here every Saturday and you buy white roses," the man said. "For you, those are free today."

"Thank you. I appreciate it."

The man wrapped the flowers in cellophane and handed them back to Philip. "They can represent purity and innocence, remembrance and sympathy. But I think these, for you, represent love and devotion."

"You're very perceptive and you're right. Thank you once again."

"No, sir. Thank *you*. See you next week."

"I don't think so."

Philip's pace slowed as he approached the grave and he took a deep breath to steady himself. He placed the white roses in front of the headstone and gently brushed his fingers across Mike's engraved name. "I miss you, Mike," he whispered. "These roses are for you. I know you've been watching over me, and you have no idea how grateful I am. I've been coming to visit every Saturday for the last six years, and each time I visit, you give me something, whether it be a thought, or a gust of wind, or just a smile, there's always something for me to take from you."

A gentle breeze rustled the leaves, as if carrying Mike's presence and the memories they shared. Philip continued, "I have good news today. I found a publisher for my novel. Remember, it started out as just a small journal and I wrote in it every day. I wrote about us mostly. The love we shared, the differences of opinion, the little quirks we possessed, like you enjoying olives and I can't stand them. That little journal has become a book. It's about time too, I guess," Philip chuckled softly. "But, there's something else." He paused; his gaze fixed on the gravestone as if seeking guidance. "I'm in love. His name is Richard. Richard Moore. Do they have last names in heaven? He's not replacing you. No one can. The truth is I'm scared. Scared of opening my heart because I promised never to fall in love, ever. But I can't keep that promise, Mike. And also, I don't want to invest myself in someone else only to lose them again."

He fell into a contemplative silence, wiped his tears, then said. "I know you would want me to find happiness, and even though Richard has flaws, like me, like you and everyone else I know, he makes me happy, and I owe it to myself to explore the possibility of a new life with him. You always said 'Love always finds a way.' You said love gives and takes and if anything were to happen to you, I should move on, find someone and start all over again. It's been hell, these last six years because I've blamed myself every day for what happened, and now I need closure." With a final glance at the gravestone, Philip whispered, "Thank you for always guiding me. I'll cherish our memories, but it's time for me to finally live and love again. It's not goodbye and maybe Richard will come with me one day. Rest easy, my love."

A moment of silence followed as Philip allowed his thoughts and emotions to settle, then planted a kiss on the gravestone, stood up, and whispered a final farewell before leaving the cemetery to meet with Emma in a cosy coffee bar.

***

Philip sat at a corner table sipping on his latte when Emma slid the chair back and joined him.

"Good morning! You look amazing as usual," he said, looking up and smiling.

"Good morning, and thank you," Emma replied. "Have you been to see Mike?"

"I just came from there."

"I take my hat off to you. Every Saturday for the last six years. That must be some kind of record."

"I think that's all done now."

"Done? What do you mean?"

"I ordered a latte for you. Hope you don't mind. These past few days have been hell and I've been doing a lot of thinking," Philip began, taking a deep breath. "Em, you're stuck with me. We've built something special together and I'm not ever going to walk away from us, or Wedding Bells."

Emma looked relieved. "I'm glad to hear."

Philip nodded, understanding her concern. "So, are we good?"

Emma smiled. "We're good, for now."

"How is Tom doing?"

Emma shrugged and pulled out a folder. She offered it to Philip and he opened it. "His first proposal. Not great I'm afraid. It's for Dylan Shaw Graphic Design."

Philip opened the folder and noticed names like the Belmond Mount Nelson Hotel, Event Couture, Blomboy, Stir Food, and Molecular Bars.

"Jesus! He's paying for names here. This will cost a fortune."

"The cost breakdown is on the next page."

"Four hundred thousand? What did the client say?"

"He wants a new proposal."

"I'll email one to you. Can I hold onto this? I'll need the rest of the brief."

"He wants the proposal by Monday morning at ten."

"You'll have it tomorrow morning. Tell me more about Tom."

"He had his own company and had to close because of COVID. I think he's a good fit but he tends to overreach."

"Are we going to keep him?"

"I think we should. I can't do it alone."

"Listen, Emma," he took her hand. "This writer's workshop isn't forever. Just another two weeks and I'll be back in the office. I'm investing more money in Wedding Bells, so neither of us are going anywhere. Remember, not even COVID could kick our arse. We pulled through that like champions."

"I can't match your investment, Philip."

"I'm not asking you to match anything. Just three weeks and I'll be back. I never want you to feel that I'm abandoning ship. Writing is part of my life and I'll be doing tours and book signings so prepare yourself. Whatever happens, you remain at the top, running the business, making decisions. That's what we wanted, remember. Just to live comfortably."

She shed a tear as she gazed at Philip. "I remember. Down and out isn't in our vocab. We've done well."

"And we'll continue to do well until *you* call it quits."

"Why me?"

Philip's gaze locked with Emma's. "Because I did this for both of us. I started this business when Mike died because I needed a fresh start. But then you came to me and said you're going back to England because there's nothing in South Africa. No money, no job, nothing. I had to act quickly. I wasn't prepared to lose my best friend then, and I'm sure as hell not going to lose her now."

"Philip, you know I've always believed in your talent as a writer. I've seen your dedication and passion. But running this business with you, creating something together, it's been more than just a job."

"We've built something that's touched the lives of so many people and I can't stop writing, Em. I'll find a way to balance both."

"That's what I've always loved about you. Your ability to dream big, to fight for what you believe in."

"And I'll always do that. Sometimes I'll lose the battle, other times I'll win. But that's to be expected."

"Tell me about Richard. Are you winning?"

He smiled, just the thought of Richard made his day worth living.

"Philip Mitchell, that smile says it all."

"I... I don't know. I fucked up badly. Accused him of being disloyal and untrustworthy. But I know it was losing Mike like that fucked me up, but he still doesn't know the full truth about that day."

"What truth?"

"That I killed Mike."

"You're full of crap, you know that? You didn't kill Mike. When will you stop with this?"

"He'd still be alive if I didn't ask him to stand in for me."

"Bullshit! I'm not going to listen to one more word of this. What did you mean when you said visiting Mike is all done?"

Philip turned his head away from Emma and found it difficult to talk through his sobbing. "I'm... I'm in love, Em. I can't stop thinking about Richard. We've spent the last few days together editing the manuscript and he's turned my life upside down."

"Are you going to tell him?"

Philip nodded. "Soon. I just don't know when."

# Chapter 22

At Cape Point, Philip stared at a photo of Mike displayed prominently on the mantel above the fireplace when June interrupted him. "You haven't said a word in ten minutes, my boy. That picture isn't going anywhere. You need to open yourself up to new possibilities and Richard deserves a chance. I've seen how he is with you. He cares about you deeply."

"I wasn't sure if I could trust him completely. He did let me down, but we all have flaws and I forgot about my own. We've spent some time together this week working on the manuscript and he doesn't know it but I couldn't really think properly while he was there. I wanted to hold him and tell him how sorry I am for pushing him away, but I just couldn't bring myself to do it, Mom. I'm possessive, jealous and even impulsive. Who wants to love someone like that? Who wants someone breathing down their neck every minute of the day? Keeping tabs on them? Testing them?"

June leaned closer, her voice gentle yet firm. "People change, Philip. You live in the past. You think that you can't and never will love anyone else because of Mike. Your thoughts feed you all that nonsense. Mike is in the past. He is *not* in your future and you need to live for now. Today. No one ever wrote a history book that deals with the future. I think that comes from Eckard Tolle. You should read his books. I'm telling you, get over Mike or you'll land up in an early grave."

"I think I'm ready, Mom."

"What, for the grave?"

"I'm ready for love. I miss it. I'm ready to put Mike in the past. Funny thing, at the cemetery this morning I told him I need to be loved."

"That's a start."

Philip sighed, contemplating his feelings for Richard. "I do want Richard. He's kind, and understanding."

June smiled, "Let me get this right. Are you in love with Richard?"

Philip's cheeks flushed, but he nodded, unable to deny the truth. "I'm in love with him, and I've been afraid to admit it."

June squeezed Philip's hand gently. "Then tell him. Life is too short to deny yourself happiness, besides, life was never meant to be lived alone."

As Philip stood up to leave, June looked at him. "Remember, you deserve to experience love fully."

# Chapter 23

Philip arrived before the sun went down and met Richard outside. Richard took his hand and kissed it gently. "I got worried you might not want to come home," he said, leading him into the cottage and straight onto the patio where he had laid out the table for dinner.

Philip's eyes grew wide. "What's this?" he said, pointing at the candle-lit table set for two. Richard pulled the chair out and gestured for Philip to sit.

"Sir, I hope you will enjoy a Richard Moore dining experience. We have fresh flowers from the dunes up the beach, and your favourite sweet wine especially collected from our local bottle store, still cold and waiting to be opened. If you will indulge me a moment longer, I'd like to present our menu, specially created with you in mind." He opened the printed, folded menu and handed it to Philip, smiling from ear to ear.

"I spent the entire day preparing this. Oh, and one other thing, music." He pressed a button on the Wi-Fi speaker control and 'One More Try' by George Michael reached out towards the shoreline.

Richard extended a hand and Philip accepted his silent request for a dance. No words were necessary as they moved to the music and gazed into each other's eyes.

"You didn't have to go all out like this," Philip said, clearly touched by the effort Richard had put into their dinner.

"I wanted to spoil you," Richard replied with a warm smile, gesturing for Philip to take a seat. "You deserve it." During the course of the dinner, Philip opened up. "I want you to know why I've been holding back in our relationship," he said softly. "It's not just because of Mike, or the guilt that's followed me for the last six years, but it's also because of who I am. I'm selfish, sometimes rude, sometimes unforgiving, and jealous and everything is all about me. I don't want to be hurt, ever again. And I don't want to hurt you."

Richard nodded, "I've been hurt too," he said, "Perhaps not in the same profound way as you. I've had my heart broken twice, each time hoping that this man would be the one, the person I could spend my life with. I long for a love that lasts, to grow old together and make the most of this one life we have."

"I feel the same way. I think about Mike's accident all the time. I haven't told you this and it's difficult but it should have been me on that plane," Philip said, hanging his head as though in shame. Thoughts of that fateful day flooded his mind.

Richard took his hand. "You don't have to go through this, Philip. Tell me when you're ready."

A knot formed in Philip's throat. "I want to. I need you to understand where my feelings go sometimes."

A lump formed in Philip's throat as he recounted the story. His voice trembling with sorrow and guilt, his emotions raw and palpable. He took a deep breath to steady himself before continuing. "I ran my small events company from here as my base of operations. And Mike would lend a hand whenever he could, assisting me when he had some free time. But that weekend... In 2017, I helped plan Cape Town's 20th anniversary of its UNESCO World Heritage Site status. I couldn't miss it; I had to be there, running the show." Philip's voice quivered as he reached the turning point. "A friend from Worcester called me on the Wednesday, just days before the event. She asked me to plan her daughter's twenty-first birthday party and she could only meet with me to plan the celebration on the coming weekend. I couldn't be in two places at the same time."

His voice choked but he continued. "The weather was clear when Mike took off. But you know how unpredictable the weather can be in Cape Town." Philip's grief erupted in uncontrollable sobs; his pain too immense to bear.

Richard held him tightly. "Philip," Richard whispered, his voice filled with compassion. "Please, don't blame yourself."

Between sobs, Philip managed to express his anguish. "I miss him every single day Richard. *I should have been on that plane with him*," he cried, his heartache pouring forth.

Richard's touch was gentle as he wiped away Philip's tears, his voice soothing. "Shh," he murmured softly. "It's not your fault," he whispered, his voice filled with compassion. "You couldn't have known."

Philip's tears subsided gradually as he absorbed Richard's comforting words. He clung to Richard, finding a place of safety and warmth in his embrace. "I... I feel responsible," he murmured. "If only I had said no to that request, if only I hadn't allowed him to fly that morning, if only I had been with him..."

Richard held Philip even tighter. "Listen to me, Philip," he said firmly, but gently. "I said this earlier, you can't blame yourself for something that was beyond your control. You had no way of foreseeing what would happen. It was an unforeseen tragedy, a cruel twist of fate."

Philip's eyes searched Richard's face, desperate for reassurance. "But I should have been there," he whispered, his voice trembling. "Mike was going in my place."

"It's natural to have those thoughts, Philip. But dwelling on 'what ifs' won't change anything. You can't rewrite the past. All you can do is honour Mike's memory, cherish the times you had with him, and find a way forward."

Philip nodded, his gaze still clouded with grief but also acceptance. "I know. You're right," he murmured, his voice quieter now. "Mike wouldn't want me to blame myself. He was always the one to bring joy and laughter, the one who would lift our spirits. I need to remember him for that, for the light he brought into our lives. Just like you are doing."

Richard said. "Remember him with love and gratitude. That's all you can do. We don't need to work on the last chapter tonight if you're not up to it. I'll phone Silas and tell him to expect it whenever."

Philip shook his head, "It's okay. I'm ready for it. Maybe that's why I couldn't do it before. I needed to dig deep down again."

"Are you sure?"

Richard brought the laptop to the patio, and side by side, they worked together. As they finished writing the final lines, they exchanged a glance, their hearts resonating with the love and hope that they had poured into their story.

"Thank you for being a part of my journey," Philip said.

Richard smiled, his eyes gleaming with affection. "It's my pleasure."

With a gentle touch, Philip closed the laptop. and reached for the bottle of champagne. With a satisfying pop, he opened it.

"To happy endings," Richard raised his glass.

"And to us," Philip replied, his voice filled with joy. His gaze locked onto Richard's and his tummy raced with butterflies.

Richard took his hand and led him onto the beach and found a spot in the quiet of the night with just the waves lapping and running up the shoreline.

Philip turned to Richard and, with a tender gesture, reached out to touch his hand. Their fingers intertwined, creating a silent bridge between their hearts. Richard moved closer, their shoulders gently brushing against each other. He raised his champagne glass to Philip's lips, offering a sip in the fading light. Philip sipped slowly and finally Richard's lips met his in a tender and heartfelt kiss. Their lips and tongues moved together in a dance of passion as they lost themselves in the intoxicating sweetness of the moment. The salty breeze from the ocean caressed their skin. It was a magical embrace, a merging of two hearts beating as one. In that single kiss, the world around them faded into insignificance, and all that mattered was the moment.

As they pulled apart, Richard smiled, "Thank you," he whispered.

"For what?"

"For confiding in me."

Philip's eyes sparkled with surprise and joy. He had never expected to open up like this, to reveal his true feelings. His heart swelled with a newfound tenderness for Richard, realising that they were both longing for the same connection. "You don't have to thank me," he whispered, his voice filled with sincerity. "I've waited a long time for us to happen. I was afraid," Philip admitted. "Afraid that if I shared my feelings, I would lose you. But I can't keep it hidden anymore. I care about you deeply, Richard."

Richard's lips curled into a gentle smile, his hand reached up to hold Philip's hand. "I don't want to lose you," Richard said.

In that moment, their fears and doubts melted away. Their journey together had just begun, and they would face challenges and uncertainties, but they were willing to embrace it all.

***

Back at the cottage Philip excused himself to shower outside. He invited Richard to join him but Richard politely refused. Instead, he watched as the warm water flowed over Philip's body, shining in the moonlight.

Philip rinsed away the soap, feeling the water flowing over his skin. As he turned his gaze towards Richard, he caught a glimpse of him quickly stepping out of sight. A playful smile crept across his face. Although Richard had politely declined the invitation, Philip couldn't ignore the bond that had formed between them. He stepped out of the shower, feeling refreshed and invigorated, wrapped a towel around his waist and went inside to find Richard reading the last page of the manuscript.

"Your turn. The water's warm"

***

Richard shut the laptop. Guilt washed over him for intruding on Philip's privacy. He undressed and entered the shower. As the water cascaded over him, Richard's mind began to wander. For a solid ten minutes, he indulged in vivid thoughts of Philip's skin against his own. With each gentle stroke of the soap, Richard embraced the sensuousness of the moment and the fantasy that danced through his mind as he cleaned himself.

After thoroughly rinsing off, he stepped out of the shower, the tantalizing imagery of Philip's nakedness still fresh in his thoughts. He dried himself off and quietly entered the bedroom.

Philip was already in bed, naked. His eyes shut tight. A duvet covered his legs and waist. Richard watched from the doorway with thoughts of how fortunate he was to have salvaged their connection from the brink of destruction, and how his body tingled when they had kissed earlier. He stood there, his hands gently encouraging his erection, pushing it to the limit. Philip's beauty supported his lust; fine hair lightly dusted his chest and arms, creating a delicate texture against his skin. Each breath accentuated the subtle rise and fall of his well-toned abdomen, revealing a set of hard, muscular abs. His arms exuded power and softness, with biceps that rippled with every breath. Veins traced their way across his forearms, adding to his physical prowess. The sight of Philip's body was captivating, a combination of strength and grace that held an undeniable allure. He moved quietly to the edge of the bed and removed his nightgown.

Philip stirred, his eyes fluttering open. Sensing Richard's presence, he turned his gaze towards him and casually removed the duvet that covered his waist, revealing his erection. Moonlight cascaded over Philip's body, accentuating the contours and curves of his thighs. The intimacy of the moment filled the room with a sexual tension that could snap at any moment.

With a look of longing in his eyes, Philip extended an unspoken invitation, and Richard accepted wholeheartedly.

He gently lowered himself to meet Philip's body and the moment their skin touched, it was like an angel singing. Philip's entire body trembled as he whispered, "I want you so much."

***

As the first rays of morning filtered through the curtains, Philip stirred from his sleep. The memories of the previous night's passion lingered, leaving him with longing and anticipation. He turned to face Richard, who was on his side, staring at him.

"You're incredibly beautiful," Richard said.

Philip smiled. "You too," he murmured, his voice filled with hope. "When will we see each other again?"

Richard's lips curled into a smile as he reached out to caress Philip's cheek. "Tonight," he replied. "I don't want to wait any longer. I want to be with you."

Philip's heart skipped a beat at Richard's words, a surge of happiness coursing through his veins. The prospect of seeing Richard again made his world a brighter, more vibrant place.

"Tonight," Philip repeated, his voice filled with anticipation and affection. "I can't wait."

Richard leaned in, capturing Philip's lips in a tender kiss. He whispered against Philip's mouth. "Until then, I miss you already."

Richard got out of bed and suddenly stopped. "Shit!"

"What's wrong?" Philip asked.

"We forgot to email Silas."

Philip leaped from the bed and sprinted to his study and booted up his laptop. Within a few minutes he hit send.

"Done," he said and didn't wait a moment longer, he leaped onto the bed beside Philip. "I can't wait to spend the day with you," he whispered, his voice brimming with affection.

"Shh," Philip said. "I need to say something and it can't wait."

Richard moved to sit on Philip's chest while Philip reached for his erection with one hand and lightly brushed his face with the other.

"I want to apologise. I treated you like shit and you stuck with me. I don't know if anyone else would have. I'm sorry."

Richard couldn't look away. "I should be the one to apologize," he said. "I should have backed off. Said no to Silas when he asked me to edit your work. I knew that if I said no, I'd have to work twice as hard to be close to you. I wanted to be with you every minute."

Philip's gaze was filled with respect. "Mine was a selfish, stupid reason. I nearly lost you."

"You'll never lose me."

Philip pulled Richard over his chest and kissed him with all the passion he had buried during those six years of torment. Richard's erection wedged against Philip's stomach and the kiss he offered was full and wet with their tongues searching for power, dancing with passion, and loving with tenderness. Their kisses turned into a passion of exploration with both men fighting for dominion across tight, muscled flesh from ears to armpits and nipples back to their mouths and at last Richard won Philip over with his tongue as it explored Philip's throbbing erection. He licked and kissed Philip's shaft from head to root and then engulfed it whole down to the back of his throat leaving trails saliva with each plunge. Philip gripped Richard's shoulders, pushing him down to take his full erection, then gripped his hair and pulled him up to meet his mouth and suck out his own precum. Richard closed his eyes, unable to tear himself away, every muscle in his body tensed as Philip used his tongue to eat Richard's treasure trail, then down between his thighs and eventually taking his scrotum into his mouth, one ball at a time, leaving Richard's golden pubic hair shiny wet. He teased Richard's erection with his teeth and tongue and eventually took it into his mouth where it slid deep. Richard groaned and suddenly withdrew.

"Easy," Richard whispered. "I don't want to cum right now."

Philip backed off and pulled Richard into a seated position where he straddled across Richard's thighs until their erections where joined. Both throbbing and yearning for release. The two men clutched each other with their erections crossing like swords, both filled with streams of precum. Richard rose up until his erection was level with Philip's mouth and Philip stared at it as though in worship before taking it gently into his mouth, devouring it, sucking beneath Richard's foreskin.

Richard pulled away again. Lovingly he searched Philip's eyes and then slowly turned him around until his ass was backed up against Richard's cock.

"I want you deep inside," Philip whispered.

"Are you sure? I don't want to hurt you," Richard said.

"I'll tell you when it hurts."

Richard licked Philip's hole until it was slippery and tender. Philip's entire body tensed up as the licking intensified.

"I need you inside me. Right now." He opened his bedside drawer and handed Richard the bottle of water-based lube. Richard applied it to the head and length of his cock and added a copious amount to Philip's hole, gently pushing the lube in with a finger.

Gently he pressed his cock into Philip's body and gracefully advanced until his entire erection had disappeared. Just as slowly, he withdrew, then repeated the process.

"Are you okay?" Richard asked, pulling him up by the shoulders and kissing Philip's neck.

Philip smiled. "It's been so long, babe. Fuck me, please fuck me," he whispered.

***

Silas's phone pinged with a notification, indicating the arrival of a new email. Curiosity and anticipation danced in his eyes as he opened the message, not quite sure what to expect. It was from Philip with an attachment and a message:

*At last, the final edit. Enjoy.*

Silas couldn't contain his joy. He let out a triumphant whoop, his excitement echoing through the room. It was as if a weight had been lifted, and his heart soared with happiness.

With a burst of energy, he dashed toward the bathroom where Jack was showering. He burst in, unable to contain his enthusiasm. "Jack!" he exclaimed, his voice filled with unbridled joy. "You won't believe it! Richard finished the edit on Philip's book!"

Startled by the sudden intrusion, Jack turned off the shower and peeked out from behind the curtain. Water dripped from his hair as his eyes met Silas's. "What? Really?" Excitement creeping into his voice.

Silas nodded vigorously, unable to suppress his beaming smile. "Philip just sent them. We finally have a product."

Jack's face lit up with astonishment. He stepped out of the shower, water droplets trailing down his skin as he reached out to Silas, their hands intertwining in a shared moment of triumph.

"It's about time," Jack marvelled, his voice filled with awe. "I can't believe it's finally here."

Silas squeezed Jack's hand. "I knew Richard would deliver," he replied.

With their hands still entwined, they made their way back to their living room, the air thick with anticipation. Silas retrieved his laptop, the prized manuscript now awaiting their undivided attention. With eager fingers, he opened the email and clicked on the attachment, revealing the final chapters they had longed for.

As they began to read, time slowed. Each word, each sentence, wove together a tapestry of emotions and revelations. They laughed, they gasped, and they shed tears as they journeyed through the conclusion of Philip's creation. The final chapters carried them through a whirlwind of emotions, leaving them breathless and satisfied.

As Silas closed the laptop, a sense of accomplishment settled upon him. He knew their work was far from over – the journey towards publication lay ahead.

He sent a quick message to both Philip and Richard. It was simple, but it meant a thousand words more:

*Thank you*

# Chapter 24

"I was thinking of starting tonight's workshop on genre with something they won't expect," Philip said. "Personally, the idea of exploring imaginative realms and breaking free from the confines of genres sparks my own creativity."

"I don't know," Richard said. "I mean, one of the first questions you should ask before you write a story or book is what genre is it? Is it horror? Crime? Romance? Each genre is formula specific."

"But that's just the beauty of it, genre doesn't need to conform. Let's say I write a romantic thriller. Is it just a thriller?"

"It's a romantic thriller."

"Exactly. I'm going to have to use all the principles that enshrine those two genres in one book. And if I want to write a romance thriller with humour then I should be able to do it, right?"

"And come up with a new formula."

"Many writers don't write according to a set formula. They just write…"

Philip didn't finish the sentence. His phone buzzed with an incoming message from Emma. "Still waiting for that proposal for Dylan," he read out loud.

Richard stepped closer, placing a comforting hand on Philip's shoulder. "Is everything alright?" he asked with genuine concern in his voice.

Philip sighed, his gaze shifting from the message to Richard. "I've been meaning to work on a proposal for Dylan Shaw Graphic Design Services. They're celebrating their fifteenth anniversary in three weeks," he explained. "But with everything going on, I haven't found the time to focus on it. It shouldn't take me long," Philip continued, his tone infused with determination.

Philip gathered the necessary materials for the proposal and for the next half hour, focused on developing a plan for the graphic design company. "She has to present this at 10.30 this morning. I can do this. Maybe even meet her at Shaw's offices."

"Sounds good to me," Richard said.

Philip took a deep breath and typed a quick response to Emma:

*I'm working on it. See you at Shaw's office at 10.15*

***

They arrived at the offices in Camps Bay just before 10.15. In Dylan Shaw's boardroom, Philip extended his hand towards Tom and said, "Good to finally meet you, Tom."

Tom shook Philip's hand with a smile. "Thank you, Philip."

Philip turned to Emma and said, "Emma, this is Richard."

Richard approached Emma, extending his hand as well. "Emma, it's a pleasure to meet you. Philip has spoken highly of you."

Emma shook Richard's hand warmly. "I saw you at Barbara's wedding but never got around to meeting you. It's great to finally meet you too. Philip and I have been friends for a long time. You and I need to chat after this meeting. Alone."

"Sure thing. I hope it's nothing bad," Richard said.

"Wait and see," Emma said, grinning.

The room buzzed with a positive energy as the team members exchanged greetings and settled in for their discussion. Dylan Shaw entered the room and greeted everyone with a curious smile. As he took his seat at the head of the table, Emma introduced him.

"So, what have you got for me this time around?"

Philip stood up and addressed the group. "Good morning, everyone. I'm Philip Mitchell, co-owner of Wedding Bells with Emma. However, during my absence, Tom here will be taking over my role as the event planner."

Dylan nodded, recognizing Tom. "Yes, we've met."

Philip took charge and said, "Let's get down to business. I've prepared a proposal for the 15th-anniversary event. Here's a summary of the key points: First, I defined the event objectives and determined its purpose. We want to celebrate the company's achievements and strengthen client relationships."

Dylan responded with enthusiasm, "Excellent. That aligns perfectly with our goals."

Philip continued, "Next, I've set the budget at R150,000, and you'll see why in a minute."

Dylan's eyes widened, expressing surprise. "That's better than the four-hundred-thousand of the previous proposal. It seems reasonable."

Philip nodded, pleased with the response. "Agreed. Now, as for the venue, I suggest Stellenbosch Gardens. It can accommodate as many guests as you will allow. And you can maximise the guest count within the budget. The event will take place on the day of the anniversary, which falls on a Thursday. Now, this is especially beneficial because Thursday is regarded as non-peak time, and hence we can negotiate better rates with the vendors."

Dylan smiled, impressed. "I like the way this man thinks."

Philip continued confidently, "Emma will collate the guest list and use digital invitations or email invites instead of costly printed materials."

Emma chimed in, "Digital invitations will save us time and money."

Philip moved on, saying, "Another task for Emma *and* Tom will be to gather sponsorships and partnerships from local businesses, including Shaw's suppliers and customers. We should approach interested parties who can contribute financially or offer discounted services in exchange for promotional opportunities."

Emma expressed optimism, "We can secure some valuable partnerships."

Philip smiled and said, "Perfect. As for the catering options I suggest buffet-style or food stations as they tend to be more cost-effective than individual plated meals."

Dylan agreed, "Makes sense. Good food without overspending."

Philip appreciated the response. "I also believe in organising interactive activities and games, including a raffle and maybe a photo booth with branded props. This will keep your guests engaged. If anyone has other ideas, please feel free to approach Mr. Shaw, Emma or Tom and make yourself heard. It makes the event more memorable and enjoyable. For promotion, we'll utilise digital channels like Facebook, Instagram, and Twitter. We'll also send out newsletters and update your company website to promote the event. Emma and Tom will encourage attendees to share their experience on social media using a dedicated event hashtag. Finally, after the event, Emma and Tom will follow up with attendees by sending personalised thank-you emails to express gratitude for their presence and help nurture client relationships."

Dylan clapped his hands. "Now *that's* what I'm talking about. Celebrating our fifteenth in style while staying true to our brand."

Philip nodded. "With this plan, I'm confident you'll have a successful and memorable event."

Dylan expressed his gratitude and said, "When can you guys get started? We have a little over two weeks"

Tom said, "Right away, Mr. Shaw."

"I don't want a detailed report on a daily basis," Dylan continued. "Email or phone me if there's a gremlin in the works, but otherwise just do it. You'll have the money in your account in three days."

After the meeting, Emma took Richard aside, finding a moment to speak with him privately. With a warm smile, she said, "So, you're the man who has stolen my best friend's heart. And you're handsome too, which is always a plus. I wonder if they still make babies like you?"

Richard chuckled, feeling a sense of warmth from Emma's words. Emma's expression turned more serious as she continued, "Now, you listen to me," she said, poking a finger into his chest. "Philip is the most wonderful man on earth. He's sentimental and worth every bit of love you can give him. I'm begging you, don't screw with his head or his heart. He's only known true love once. You can give him a second chance."

Richard's smile softened, understanding the sincerity in Emma's words. "I can assure you I care deeply for Philip. I would never do anything to hurt him. I want to make him happy, and I understand the responsibility that comes with that."

"Caring deeply is not enough. I want to know if you're in love with him, if not, don't waste his time."

"I love him so much it hurts."

"Have you told him?"

"He knows."

"I don't care how you get the courage to tell him, but you had better do it soon. Don't play with him."

As they walked away from each other, Emma called out to remind him; "Remember what I said, Richard. Don't fuck it up. Tell him!"

***

For lunch, Philip took Richard to Reef and Sea, a restaurant known for its seafood dishes. They settled down at a table and placed their orders. However,

Richard's mind was preoccupied by Emma's words earlier. Philip noticed Richard's change in demeanour and curiosity got the better of him.

"What did Emma say to you earlier?"

Richard shrugged, trying to downplay the situation. "It was nothing, really. She just expressed happiness that we're together."

Philip sensed there was more to it and before he could inquire further, Richard's phone buzzed. He excused himself from the table to take the call. On the other end of the line, Jesse expressed his frustration. "Richard, where have you been? You haven't come home!"

Richard replied, annoyed, "I've had other things on my mind, Jesse. Important things."

Jesse inquired further, "Is it Philip?"

Richard hesitated for a moment before admitting, "Yes."

Jesse said, "I thought so, but right now, I really need you. Andrew is stuck in Bloemfontein, and he needs to be picked up immediately. I'll pay for the trip, whatever it takes."

Suddenly, Richard was torn between his responsibilities and his commitment to Philip. He broke into a cold sweat. He had not told Philip he was a pilot.

"I can't do it right away, but I'll make arrangements to fetch him tomorrow night."

"He needs to come back today."

"Today is impossible. I'm in the middle of something. It will have to wait until tomorrow night."

"It will take you four hours to get him back. *Four hours.*"

"I thought you two had broken up?"

"We did, but he's still my husband and he needs me. Please, I beg you."

"I'll see what I can do."

Richard returned to the table and hurriedly said, "Something's come up, Philip. I have to go. I'm sorry."

"What is it, Rich? Can I help?"

"A friend needs me to help him with something. It won't take long. I'll see you tonight at Llandudno."

After Richard's abrupt departure, Philip was left bewildered, trying to make sense of the situation. Something didn't add up, and he couldn't shake the feeling there was more to the phone call than met the eye. In his rush to leave the restaurant, Richard had left his cell phone on the table. Philip picked it up just as a message came through.

It was from Jesse:

*I'll meet you at Camps Bay airfield in twenty minutes.*

Without wasting a moment, Philip hurriedly made his way to his car and started the engine and the moment he arrived at the airfield, his heart sank as he realised the gravity of the situation.

He observed Richard disappearing into a nearby hangar, only to reappear moments later with Jesse beside him, holding his hand. His eyes widened as Richard approached a light aeroplane parked outside the hangar.

As Philip watched in disbelief, Richard carefully inspected the aircraft, displaying a familiarity and confidence Philip had seen before, with Mike. Without hesitation, Richard climbed into the pilot's seat and turned the ignition.

Philip's day had swiftly turned into a living nightmare. Fear gripped his heart as he stood there, his eyes glued to the plane as it started up and taxied down the runway then ascending into the sky.

As the light aircraft disappeared, Philip's joy sank into a mire of sadness. How could he not know that Richard was a pilot? How had he missed it?

# Chapter 25

Instead of heading home to Llandudno, Philip made his way to the Wedding Bells' offices. Emma and Tom were engrossed in planning the Dylan Shaw event. Emma immediately sensed something was wrong. Reacting quickly, she instructed Tom to prepare a strong cup of coffee for Philip.

"Philip, please, tell me what's wrong. I can see something is really bothering you."

Philip remained silent, lost in his thoughts. Emma assumed Richard was the cause of his distress and continued to implore Philip to open up.

"Is it about Richard? Philip, talk to me."

Reluctantly, Philip's emotions overwhelmed him, and in gasps between sobs, he finally revealed what had transpired. "Richard is not just a teacher. He's... he's also a pilot."

Emma's eyes widened with surprise; shock grasped at her body. "A pilot? Oh, shit."

Philip's voice trembled as he continued, tears streaming down his face. "I saw him... at the Camps Bay airfield holding hands with Jesse, his friend. He was supposed to spend the day with me. They climbed into some light aircraft and took off."

Emma's expression shifted from surprise to concern as she realised the impact of this revelation. "Maybe there's a perfect explanation."

Philip's shoulders shook with each sob, his voice choking with pain. "I tried to let go of Mike and not dwell on the past but I can't bear the thought of getting involved with a pilot, not after what happened to Mike."

Emma stepped closer to him, placing a comforting hand on his arm. "I understand your fears, Philip. Maybe there's more to this story you don't know yet. You can't let your past dictate your present."

"He's a fucking pilot!" Philip exploded.

She cradled him in her arms. "Richard deserves a chance to explain and you need to hear him out."

As the afternoon progressed, Philip's phone buzzed repeatedly with messages from an unknown number. Assuming it was Richard attempting to reach out through Jesse's phone, Philip made a deliberate choice to ignore them, unable to confront the situation just yet.

Emma noticed Philip's phone lighting up with notifications. "Philip, your phone is going off. Shouldn't you check who's trying to reach you?"

Philip was conflicted, but remained firm in his decision. "I can't. Not now."

The messages continued to pour in, each one growing more urgent and pleading. Philip's heart ached, knowing Richard was desperately trying to reach him. However, he couldn't bring himself to respond.

Four hours later, just when Philip was leaving the office for his workshop, his phone chimed with one final message.

Emma noticed the intensity in Philip's gaze. "What's wrong, Philip? What does the message say?"

Philip hesitated, his voice filled with conflict and uncertainty. "It's from Richard. He's at my cottage, waiting for me to come home."

"I know it's difficult, but he's there, waiting for you. Maybe it's time to face it head-on, to find the answers you need."

"I have to get to the workshop first. I have a feeling he won't be there tonight."

# Chapter 26

Philip went straight from Emma to the workshop venue and began his lecture on Genre and Setting. Richard's seat was empty and Philip had to suppress any visible display of emotion.

"Tonight, I'm focusing on genre and setting. But, before I carry on, I want you to remember this: focus on strong storytelling regardless of the genre, remember, a compelling story with well-developed characters, a well-paced plot, and engaging writing is crucial. Genre provides a framework but it's ultimately the strength of your storytelling that will captivate readers... "

The door to the auditorium opened and Philip stopped talking, only for a moment, as Richard made his way to his seat.

"Familiarise yourself with different genres: Take the time to research and understand them. Romance, mystery, science fiction, fantasy, historical fiction, thriller, and more. Read widely in each genre to gain a deeper understanding of their characteristics and storytelling techniques. By doing this, you'll be better placed to write a compelling story."

As the workshop came to a close, the room emptied, leaving Richard and Philip alone with their unresolved emotions. Philip handed Richard his forgotten cell phone. "You left this at the restaurant."

Richard took the phone and slipped it into his shirt pocket, his eyes filled with remorse. "I'm so sorry, Philip," he murmured, his voice barely above a whisper.

"Sorry? Sorry for what, Richard? You lied to me. When were you going to tell me?" Philip's voice cracked with emotion.

Richard's gaze dropped, and he spoke with a heavy heart. "I didn't want to tell you because I knew what you had gone through with Mike. Pilots. Light aircraft. Heartbreak. I didn't want to hurt you."

Philip's voice trembled as he expressed his feelings. "Were you ever going to tell me? Or was I *supposed* to find out on my own?"

Richard's voice softened, filled with regret. "I wanted to tell you several times but chickened out. I would have told you. I wanted to find the right time."

Philip's face contorted with pain and resignation. "But *you know*, Richard. *You know* I could never get involved with a pilot. It's just too close to home," he said, his voice choked with emotion.

"I tried to tell you. Not once, but twice. I knew you'd take it like this so I kept quiet." Tears welled up in Richard's eyes as he struggled with his conflicting emotions. "Jesse asked me to help him fetch his husband from Worcester because he was stranded there. I couldn't say no."

"And I guess you hold hands with all your friends."

"I've known Jesse a long time. He's like a brother to me."

Philip took a deep breath, trying to compose himself, but the pain in his heart was overwhelming. "It's not just about holding hands, Richard," he said, his voice wavering.

"I understand. I really do," he said, his voice full of remorse. "But you also know how much flying means to me. Writing is *your* passion. Flying is *mine*."

Philip turned away, tears streaming down his cheeks. "I can't ask you to give up your passion, Richard. I just can't bear the thought of losing someone else I love because of flying."

Richard's heart sank, torn between his love for Philip and his love for flying. "I don't know what to do," he admitted, his voice cracking. "I never wanted to hurt you, but I can't ignore my love for flying either. It's who I am."

Philip turned back to face him, his eyes red and swollen. "I don't want to hold you back," he said, his voice barely audible. "If flying is truly what makes you happy, then maybe we just aren't meant to be together."

"*You* make me happy, Philip."

There was a long, heavy silence between them as they both grappled with the difficult decision they faced. Finally, Philip spoke, his voice steady but filled with sadness. "Maybe it's time for us to go our separate ways," he said, his words feeling like a knife to his own heart. "We can't change who we are or what we love."

Richard nodded, his heart breaking as he realized the truth in Philip's words. "Please don't kick me out of your life. There must be another way."

Philip's voice turned cold as he gathered his belongings from the podium. "I just don't see it, Richard."

"Please. We've just found each other. Please don't end it this way."

Philip brushed past him, heading towards the exit. Desperate to salvage their connection, Richard reached out, gripping Philip's elbow and spinning him around to face him.

"I love you," Richard said. His eyes were red with pain and tears.

"I love you too. But I can't bear the thought of another tragedy in my life."

With a heavy heart, Philip gently freed himself from Richard's grasp and walked away. Richard watched the love he had hoped to build slip through his fingers. He sank to his knees, and through gagging sobs, begged the universe to send Philip back to him.

# Chapter 27

Devastated and heartbroken, Richard watched Philip walk away, filled with a profound sense of loss and regret. His declaration of love could not overcome Philip's deep-seated fear and pain. He grappled with feelings of guilt and self-blame, questioning whether he should have been more honest.

In the days and weeks that followed. Memories of their time together haunted him, making it difficult to focus on anything else. He couldn't escape the thoughts of what could have been. His friends tried their best to support him, but the pain was something he had to endure alone. He often found himself looking at old photographs, rereading old messages, and replaying their last conversation in his mind, trying to find answers or some way to mend the shattered pieces of his heart.

At times, he felt an overwhelming desire to reach out to Philip, to explain himself once more, to try and make him understand the depth of his love and commitment, but his calls and messages went unanswered.

In an attempt to distract himself, he threw himself into teaching and learned to carry the memories of their love with him, cherishing the time they had spent together while acknowledging they had chosen different paths.

He stopped attending the workshop out of respect for Philip's decision. He would not embarrass Philip with his presence. He stopped making contact with June because she'd try her level best to reconcile them.

Philip had let him go.

# 3 Months Later

Emma rushed into Philip's office waving the Cape Herald in the air. "You're front-page news!" she sang and slid the paper across his desk.

Philip read the headline:

**South African Author Makes Waves with Debut Novel.**

'Born in Cape Town, Philip Mitchell has hit gold with his debut blockbuster, "Final Flight" and has been hailed as the next Nicholas Sparks. His publisher, Bolt Publishing, has planned launches at Exclusive Books and the Central News Agency throughout the country and the launch date has been set for the 12th August, just a week away. Included in the hype is the fact that Mitchell is in his late twenties and is related to one-hit-wonder, Margaret Mitchell, author of 'Gone with the Wind'. Pre-order sales have broken records throughout the country, propelling his book to number one in only a week since the book went online, surpassing Prince Harry's book in a matter of hours.'

A suave photograph of him held up the hard cover.

"How much did you say they advanced you?" Emma said, smiling.

"It's not about the advance anymore. It's about royalties now."

"Royalties or not, we're going to have to employ a receptionist because my phone, and Tom's phone has been ringing off the hook. Everyone wants to use our services and I can't cope."

"Let's start interviewing."

"Are you serious? I mean we're going to need at least two more event planners, a receptionist and someone to make us tea."

"Have you started yet?"

"What? Making tea?"

"Interviewing."

"I'll get onto it asap. Oh, your mom called while you were busy with the bishop."

"That reminds me, the bishop wants us to organise the entire African Bishops Conference in six months. Budget undisclosed, but apparently he has an open cheque."

"You didn't hear what I said, Philip."

"My mom phoned."

"She wants to see you before the book launch. Actually, she wants you there tomorrow for lunch."

"I'll talk to her tonight."

"How do you feel?"

"Nervous as hell."

"That's a good thing."

"Oh, and Richard phoned too. I told him you were occupied and couldn't be disturbed. Do you miss him?"

"You're fishing, Em."

Emma stood up and crossed the floor to the door. "I wish you weren't so stubborn, Philip. You won't take his calls and so he calls the office number sometimes twice a week. Speak to him for crying out loud!"

"The next time he calls, put him through."

That evening, while holding a glass of wine in one hand, he sat on his patio, watching the night sky. Riccardo Polidoro's 'I Surrender', played softly from his TV, streaming on YouTube. He remembered Emma's words: Speak to him for crying out loud! He lifted his cell phone and typed in Richard's number and just as quickly cancelled the call. His actions reflected the conflicting emotions swirling in his heart. He longed to reach out but he feared the unknown. What if Richard had lost interest in him? What if he had found a new man? After all, it had been three months.

He had finally let go of Mike. He didn't have to fear romance because it filled one's life with hope and love, something Richard had shown him all too often.

He punched in June's number instead, and waited for her to answer.

"It's me."

"Hi angel. I can see your name on my screen. How have you been?"

"Faring well. Nervous about the launch, but coping."

"Isn't it exciting? You're famous now. By the way, I pre-ordered ten copies of your book, just thought you might like to know."

"You shouldn't have, Mom. I get them free. You could have asked me."

"I could have, but at least I know I helped make it a bestseller. Now, tomorrow I'm having lasagne and salad, just the way you like it and since your dad's gone fishing with that man from Spain, I thought you'd like to come over. It's not a lot to ask from my own son."

"Mom, it's Tuesday tomorrow, you know I'll be there. Just no tricks this time."

"No tricks. I promise. Just be here at six on the dot."

"I'll be there. Love you."

"Love you more."

***

June did have another surprise in store. The sorrow in Philip's voice had not escaped her. It had been a full three months since Philip's fallout with Richard, and the situation needed resolve. The clock was ticking, especially with Philip's book set to be published soon. Despite her attempt to reach out to Richard by phone going unanswered, June wasn't deterred. As she sipped the last drop of her wine, she decided to pay Richard a visit at his school the following day.

She stood beside her car in the school's parking lot, anxiously awaiting Richard's arrival, and, as soon as he emerged from his vehicle, she swiftly closed the distance between them and crossed her arms, her expression a mix of concern and determination.

"June! How have you been?" Richard greeted, a hint of surprise in his voice.

"It's been an agonizing three months since we last connected," June replied.

"I know, time got away from me. I've been caught up with work," Richard explained.

"I just wish you had reached out when things took a downturn. I could have helped mend the bridge between you and Philip."

"Frankly, Philip and I have moved on from each other. He made his choice, and I respect it. There wasn't much else I could do," Richard admitted. "How's Mr. Mitchell doing?"

"He's his usual self, off on one of his fishing trips."

"Some things never change."

June sighed, "Richard, I understand you and Philip have your differences, but there's still hope. And he's on the cusp of a big moment with his book being published. It would mean a lot to him if you could find it in yourself to reconcile."

Richard's expression grew contemplative. "I don't get it, June. It would mean a lot to him, or to you?"

"It would mean a lot to me. I want you as a son-in-law. I've always wanted that from the moment I met you."

"He ignores my calls. Won't respond to my messages. I don't have a rat's ass chance."

"Is that all you've done? Sent him messages? Phoned him? What about physically facing him?"

"Not going to happen."

"At the end of the day, all friendships are worth mending. Philip's coming for dinner tonight. I want you there too. But I want to talk to you first."

Richard's gaze held hers for a moment. "I have nothing planned for tonight. What time should I be there?"

"Around five." A smile lit up June's face. "Thank you, Richard. It means a lot to me. As she turned to leave, she said, "You've changed. I like your beard. I think Philip will too."

***

Richard arrived at Cape Point one hour before Philip. He and June strolled hand in hand along a wooden path bordered by fynbos on both sides, eventually settling on a bench at the end.

The wind chilled June's ears and she leaned towards him. "Help me cover my ears with my beanie, Richard. This wind is making them cold."

He adjusted the beanie's flap over her ears and shielded it further with her yellow hoodie.

"Philip needs you," she said.

"How would you know?"

"He loves you. And don't ask me how I know that. It's a mother thing. But I can only guess that you love him too."

Richard leaned back against the bench. "I do love him, June. But I let him down. Twice. The publisher approached me to edit his work, but Philip was adamant about not letting anyone touch his manuscript. I agreed to do it, and I lost him for a moment, then he found out I fly light planes and that was it. The end. I would even give up flying if it meant spending more time with him. It's been three months now. I've phoned and left messages but he doesn't respond."

"Today it ends. You need to have an open and honest conversation with Philip. It needs to be done," she said.

He shook his head, tears welling in his eyes. "I don't know if it will work."

"Oh, Richard. It's never easy, but at least he knows you fly. If you truly love him, you need to fight for him. Challenge him. Take a moment to gather your thoughts and summon the courage. Use this opportunity, or it will be lost." June said, wiping away his tears, "My precious boy, I feel for you. But you know me. I always have a plan. Now, you'd best move your car before Philip gets here."

***

Philip arrived just before sunset and, as he entered the house, June greeted him with unabashed excitement, waving a newspaper in her hands. "Philip, look at this! You're going to take the literary world by storm!" she exclaimed, her eyes sparkling with pride.

"I know, the press is going crazy. I deliberately stayed away from reading any of it to keep my sanity," he confessed.

"They say you're better than Nicholas Sparks." she exclaimed, her excitement contagious.

Philip chuckled, "I hope I can live up to that. Right now, though, I need to focus on delivering the remaining two books to complete my contract with Bolt. There's still a lot of work ahead."

"I love the bit about you being related to Margaret Mitchell. The news is buzzing with your connection to her."

"I thought the publishers were kidding when they said they'd use that angle."

"It's all about sales, kiddo. Nothing more, nothing less. Anyway, I'm proud of you. Your dad is too. Have you eaten? I have lasagne and salads."

"Lasagne is just what the doctor ordered."

June set the table on the patio and said, "Yesterday, thirty, maybe forty dolphins passed this way. It was just incredible." She placed a plate in front of him and continued, "Have you heard from Richard?"

"I've not spoken to Richard in three months."

145

"You know how he feels about you."

"I'm sure he's found someone else. Someone else to lie to."

"Lie? Oh, I don't know about that, son."

"If he'd been honest from the get go, maybe things would have been different."

June, wise and caring, had some pearls of wisdom to share with her son. She said, "It's about Mike, isn't it? The last time we spoke you had come to terms with his death. But, you haven't, have you? I want you to listen carefully. Maybe I should have told you this a long, long time ago. In life, nothing is guaranteed. Mike came into your life to teach you a lesson — to accept things as they are and not dwell on the past or the future but recognize the present. Your relationship with Richard is a consequence of that lesson. Just because he also flies 'planes doesn't mean it's the end of the world. Has he tried contacting you?"

"Several times. But I haven't returned his calls. I wanted to last night, but just couldn't."

June reached out and held Philip's hand gently. "Well, he's been in touch with me. Richard loves you deeply. He told me he would give up flying to spend just one more minute with you. Now, if he's willing to make such sacrifices, then why don't you?"

"He never once came to see me after we broke up. Isn't that reason enough to forget him?"

"He sent you messages. Phoned you. You never responded."

"Yes, but he never *came* to me. All I wanted was for him to knock on my door, but he didn't."

Looking deeply into Philip's eyes, June asked the question that had lingered in both their hearts. "Philip, did you ever really love Richard?" she asked.

"I fell in love with Richard at Emma's wedding. I've loved him ever since, but you are right, Mom. I'm scared that what happened to Mike will happen to Richard."

June's eyes filled with compassion. They sat in silence for a moment. Eventually, she said, "Relationships can be complicated, filled with ups and downs. Sometimes, we need time and space to sort through our emotions. Mike was your first relationship. You never played the field before or after. Your dad and I didn't have to take you aside and explain the consequences of unprotected sex because to us, you were mature enough to know. Society's expectations can sometimes overshadow what we truly want, making it hard to explore new avenues. But now you have the opportunity to experience a new life with Richard. Take it, Philip. You should have knocked on his door, not the other way around."

Philip's heart was unsure of the path ahead. "I know," he said, his voice quivering with uncertainty. "It's just... I'm feeling so overwhelmed right now. I never expected things to become so complicated between Richard and myself."

"It's not complicated! You love him, he loves you. What's the complication? This fear you have that the same thing will happen to him, that's an excuse. If you want him in your life you need to tell him and be done with it."

Philip glanced up, his eyes searching for answers in June's comforting gaze. "I'm sure he doesn't love me now..."

A soft voice came from behind. Its gentle words caught Philip by surprise. "I love you more now than ever before. Not one day goes by that I don't think of you. I took you for granted. I'm sorry. "

Philip's heart skipped a beat as he swung around, his eyes widening in disbelief. His chair toppled backward as he leaped up, his feet carrying him into Richard's waiting arms. Time stood still as they embraced, holding onto each other as if they would never let go.

June left the patio and watched from inside the house. This was the moment she had hoped for, the rekindling of a love that had never waned.

Tears streamed down Philip's face as he clung to Richard, his voice choking with emotion. "Oh my God!" he cried out. "Oh my God, it's so good to hold you. I missed you so much. I'm so sorry."

Richard's embrace tightened; his own tears mingled with Philip's. "Shh," he whispered. "We've both made mistakes, but what matters is we've found our way back to each other."

As they held each other, they wiped away the tears that had fallen during their emotional reunion. Finally, they pulled apart, breathless but filled with a newfound hope.

To their surprise, June stood behind them, holding two glasses of wine in her hands. A mischievous smile danced on her lips as she extended the glasses.

"Let's celebrate," she declared, her voice filled with delight.

Philip's eyes sparkled with amusement as he looked at June, "You planned this, didn't you?"

June chuckled softly, her eyes shining with maternal pride. "Of course, I did," she confessed, her tone warm and loving. "My son deserves the very best in life, and Richard is the epitome of the very best."

****

The following day at Llandudno they strolled along the beach before heading to the cottage. Philip reached into his pocket and retrieved a set of keys. "For you," he said, opening his hand.

Richard's eyes widened, his heart skipping a beat at the gesture. "Are you sure?"

"More than ever."

Richard's eyes shimmered with unshed tears as he took the keys from Philip's outstretched hand, their fingers brushing against each other. "Thank you," Richard said, kissing Philip gently.

"The only question I have is when will you move in? Before you answer, just know I need you here like now."

"Then I'm not going to leave. You're stuck with me."

"I know, because if there's anything I've learnt this week it's that life was never meant to be lived alone."

"What about Mike's memory?"

"Sometimes I wish I could just let the wind sweep the memories away. What about you? Mom said you're prepared to give up flying."

"I will, on one condition..."

****

"I don't have a damned clue how you managed to manipulate me into this," Philip grumbled. The suffocating fumes of aviation fuel on the tarmac intensified his unease, sending a chill down his spine. Standing beside Richard's sleek light plane, the metallic gleam of its wings mocking his trepidation, Philip's heart raced like a wild stallion. A mirthless chuckle escaped his lips, a feeble attempt to cloak his fear. "I'm shitting myself," he admitted.

"I know the feeling. Each nerve in your body is jangling. Come on, babe, you've flown before. It's not all bad," Richard said.

Reluctantly, Philip took a step forward, his legs as heavy as lead. "Not since Mike." The world around him blurred as he reluctantly climbed aboard.

As Philip and Richard soared through the skies above Cape Town, a sense of awe enveloped them. The vibrant cityscape sprawled beneath them, the ocean shimmering in the distance. The wind whistled through the open cockpit, tousling their hair and bringing a tingling sensation to Philip's skin. The scent of the salty sea air mingled with the earthy aroma of the surrounding landscape. The bustling streets below them, now mere specks against the backdrop of the majestic Table Mountain. With each dip and turn of the plane a new vista opened. Here Philip watched a shoal of dolphins skipping across the Atlantic, there he noticed the line that separated the Atlantic from the Indian ocean. The golden beach of Sandy Bay sprawled below, and just for comfort, Richard flew over Llandudno. On their return to Camps Bay, the rocky towers of The Twelve Apostles seemed to reach out and grab them. In that boundless sky, Philip's love for Richard expanded like the horizon stretching out over the two oceans.

# Epilogue

The grand ballroom of the Mount Nelson Hotel buzzed with excitement as guests arrived, adorned in their finest attire, eager to get their hands on the book that had been touted as a must-read by the great-great grandnephew of Margaret Mitchell.

The venue, adorned with tasteful decorations, had a banner proudly displaying the title of the book, 'Final Flight,' with the words, 'Sunday Times Bestselling Author' across the foyer. Guests mingled, sipping on glasses of sparkling champagne and engaging in conversations about the release in almost every bookshop around the world.

Richard stood tall beside Philip, both wearing sharp black suits and black bowties. They moved through the gathering with graceful strides and caught the attention of those around them. Richard's white-blond hair swayed slightly with each step. His silver eyes sparkled with an infectious energy, captivating the gaze of onlookers. Philip's blue eyes held a glimmer of warmth and kindness as he spoke to guests who approached. Philip was mesmerised every time Richard greeted a lady; his subtle inclination, the slight lean, his lips lightly brushing against their hands with a graceful reverence.

Philip greeted each guest with a warm smile and a signed copy of his book, expressing his gratitude for their support. Cameras flashed, capturing the essence of the event and preserving the memories for future recollection. Journalists and reporters swarmed around, eager to interview him, seeking insights into his creative process and the inspiration behind the captivating story.

As the evening progressed, Philip took the stage, and tapped the microphone to test the sound.

"One thing my father taught me at a very young age was to never blow into a microphone," he smiled. "I had a book written with my speech but thought it best to just say what I really feel so it won't be long. Bolt Publishing accepted my manuscript within twelve hours of receiving it. If they hadn't, I would never have had the opportunity of working with Richard Moore during the editing process. It's a magical thing when a publisher invests in an unknown author with a debut book. I'll never forget that day."

With each word he spoke, the audience was captivated, hanging on to his every sentence. "The book actually found me. Six years ago, I lost my husband in an aeroplane crash. That's not all I lost; also hope, and I questioned life. I was lost. This book turned that all around. Writing it taught me how to love again. It showed me the way home. It made me realise that there are people in my life whom I cherish beyond all words. June, my mother, full of worldly advice. Emma, my best friend and business partner who never gave up on me even when the business had no direction, Silas Turner from Bolt Publishing who pushed me to madness, and Richard Moore, my editor and fiancé, the man I fell in love with during the run-up to the book's launch. Without you guys I would still be wallowing in self-pity, so I thank you all. And thank you to my readers, without you this book would mean nothing. That's it. Please enjoy the evening. Oh and, there are no refunds so don't even try."

A thunderous applause erupted. Guests approached him, eagerly awaiting their turn to have their books signed, their faces beaming with excitement and admiration.

***

At six in the morning, Philip and Richard found a moment together without crowds of people around them. They had removed their ties and unbuttoned their shirts and now sat side by side on the beach at Llandudno, their feet sinking into the warm sand.

The coolness of the morning enveloped them as birds chirped and seagulls called out to each other. The beach stretched up the coastline, deserted and serene. Crashing waves rushed in and then retreated. Suddenly, Richard pulled Philip up, urging him towards the water's edge. Philip eventually yielded when he saw Richard heading into the water.

"The water's freezing," Philip cried out.

"It's Cape Town, what do you expect?" Richard replied, laughing as he undressed down to his boxers.

Philip unclothed himself completely. They splashed around in the shallows, their laughter blending with the sound of the waves. They hugged, embraced and kissed and in a tender moment, Richard whispered into Philip's ear, "Will you be my husband?"

Philip's eyes widened in disbelief, his heart racing. "What did you just say?"

"I asked you to marry me."

Philip responded with a gentle kiss, tears of joy streaming down his face.

"Is that a yes?" Richard asked.

"What do you think? Of course, it's a yes!"

Richard revealed a platinum ring he had tightly held in his hand all this time, and slipped it onto Philip's ring finger.

"When did you decide this?"

Richard gazed into Philip's eyes. "The night I met you at Barbara's wedding."

"You're kidding! That night I couldn't keep my eyes off you and I thought, ag, he's as straight as a dye. You didn't look at me once."

"I know you were staring. Whenever you looked away, your mom would tell me and that's when I looked. Strange how things happen. You were thinking I wasn't interested and I was thinking of marrying you right there and then...

The early morning bliss was shattered by Richard's phone ringing on the beach close to the cottage.

"Who could that be at this ungodly hour?" Richard asked. Perplexed, they stepped out of the water and Richard picked up his phone to check the message. "It's a message from your mom."

*He said yes, didn't he?*

End

# Find me online:

Lee Quail - Facebook[1]
Lee's Works - quailsretreat.blogspot.com[2]

---

1. https://www.facebook.com/lee.quail.12/

2.     https://quailsretreat.blogspot.com/p/the-works.html

# Dedication

For David Blyth
and
Coy Luke Turner

# Don't miss out!

Visit the website below and you can sign up to receive emails whenever Lee Quail publishes a new book. There's no charge and no obligation.

https://books2read.com/r/B-A-GNMEB-KRSHD

Connecting independent readers to independent writers.

# Also by Lee Quail

**Raw Instinct**
Raw (Round 1)


**Standalone**
Love, Planes, & Heartache
Searching for Love on the Moon
The Sky in his Eyes
That Little Book Shop in Rome where it's Easy to Murder Someone


Watch for more at https://www.facebook.com/lee.quail.12.

# About the Author

Lee Quail (1993) was born in Johannesburg, South Africa, to British immigrant parents. His first book, "Gideon," was published via Amazon on 21 December, 2018. He lives with his two extremely cocky Yorkies and sometimes mows the lawn between writing. He is also a graphic designer, cooks his own food, cuts his own hair and buys his own clothes. He lives in the first house ever built in his area in the 60's.

Read more at https://leequail29.wixsite.com/lee-quail.